Chocolate Cake with Hitler

Chocolate Cake with Hitler

EMMA CRAIGIE

First published in 2010 by
Short Books
3A Exmouth House
Pine Street
EC1R 0JH

10 9 8 7 6 5 4 3

A CIP catalogue record for this book
is available from the British Library.

ISBN 978-1-906021-89-4

Cover photograph © Getty Images

Printed and bound by CPI Group (UK) Ltd, Croydon, CR0 4YY

This book is in memory of Stan Craigie

'Only the oldest, Helga, sometimes had a sad,
knowing expression in her big brown eyes...
sometimes I think, with horror, that in her heart that
child saw through the pretence of the grown-ups.'
Traudl Junge, *Until the Final Hour*

'Children's experiences deserve to be understood
across the racial and national divides, not because of their simi-
larities but because their extreme contrasts help us to see the
Nazi social order as a whole. Children were neither just the
mute and traumatised witnesses to this war, nor merely its
innocent victims. They also lived in the war, played and fell in
love during the war; the war invaded their imaginations and the
war raged inside them.'
Nicholas Stargardt, *Witnesses of War*

'The reader may ask how to tell fact from fiction.
A rough guide: anything that seems particularly unlikely
is probably true.'
Hilary Mantel, *A Place of Greater Safety*

1936

I'M SITTING WITH Papa on a bench beside the sea. I must be about three years old. The sun is in my eyes. There's a man in a white hat taking photographs. Papa is laughing. The breeze is puffing his white shirt but I'm warm because of the sun and because I'm leaning right into Papa and his arm is firmly around me. I'm as comfortable as can be and it's as if I realise for the first time that Papa is special. He is not just someone in the background. He is here and I am safe with him.

The moment is quickly over. Uncle Leader, who has been watching us, says "My turn!" and Papa leaps off the bench and Uncle Leader sits down beside me. He wants his photograph taken with me too. I hardly know Uncle Leader. He sits right up next to me, and I have to swing my leg away and across my other leg so that he's not touching. I know he wants to put his arm around me like Papa. He's breathing over me, and I try to ignore him.

"You, Helga Goebbels, are my favourite girl in the whole world. If only you were twenty years older!"

The man in the white hat is laughing. Papa is laughing. I am not going to take any notice. Uncle Leader leans closer, his smell like the furniture in the servants' quarters. I can pretend he's not there. I turn right away and stare at the camera.

I think this is my earliest memory.

I am sitting in a high chair and Mummy is sitting on a chair facing me. She is leaning forward and holding both my hands in one of hers. In the other hand she has a spoon which she's bringing towards me through the air.

"Choo, choo," she says brightly. "Here comes the train. Here comes the train."

On the spoon is a wobbling grey blob. It smells like the old cloths Cook boils up on the stove. I know the train trick and when the metal spoon reaches my mouth I keep my lips tightly shut. Mummy presses the spoon against them and I shake my head in an attempt to fend it off. "Come on, Helga, here comes the train. The train wants to come into the station." She's squashing my hands. The metal of the spoon is jamming against my lips. I will not open my mouth. I will not open my mouth. The spoon presses harder and I taste the damp, soapy paste. Mummy pushes the spoon in. A grainy lump hits the back of my throat. I retch and spit.

<hr />

I'm in a white dress with short sleeves. My sister Hilde is wearing a nicer one. Hers has a dark pink sash and little pink rosebuds around the bottom. My dress is plain, my arms are cold and my feet hurt in my gleaming new patent leather shoes.

We are in an enormous room with a sky-high ceiling.

You could pack about a million people in here – all the cheering crowds in the square outside – if they stood on each other's shoulders or lay down on top of each other like sardines but there are only a few shiny guests so it feels quite empty. Men in uniforms, ladies in hats and heels. I can't see any other children.

We join a queue to shake hands with Uncle Leader. It is his birthday. I don't want to shake his hand. I've done it before and I know it feels like a dead slug. Hilde is in front of me, littlest first. Lucky Helmut has been left at home because he's just a baby. Hilde doesn't mind, though. She shakes his hand and does a big toppling curtsy and sets off smartly for the cakes. And now it's my turn. My best bet is not to look at him. Papa is behind me, hands folded patiently, with a fake ha-ha-ha-isn't-she-a-one smile on his face. I step sideways and look out at the room. I can see the long table of cakes, the big windows, the golden chandeliers. There's a band playing outside. I hold my arms together in front of my chest so that Uncle Leader can't take my hand. He bends down towards me. Cabbagey breath. I'm backed up against the wall. Everyone is waiting for me. I make my move quickly – a bob of a curtsy – I don't even glance at him – and speed off after Hilde. She has reached the cakes. I'm just deciding whether to go for the chocolate layer cake or a gingerbread heart when Papa comes up beside us. He's not laughing now; his cheeks are peeled back in a toothy smile. He bends

down and whispers in my ear.
"Rude girls don't get cakes."

━━━━━━━━━━━━━━━━━

Day One in the Bunker
Sunday 22 April, 1945

I am lying on a bottom bunk with Heide who has finally fallen asleep next to me with her head nestled in my armpit and her feet on top of my shins. I'm never going to get to sleep like this. We're pitched in together because the mattress has a ravine in the middle. The imprint of all the soldiers who have slept here before us. No one else would share with Heide because she wriggles. There are only two bunk beds between the six of us – Hedda is above us and Hilde is above Holde and Helmut is on a blanket on the floor. He's delighted. When we realised that there weren't enough beds for us he declared, "All German people have to make sacrifices in the hour of darkness." He's always pretending to be like Papa. Anyway, he managed to fall straight to sleep which is pretty incredible considering there's only a thin army blanket between him and the concrete floor. Mummy says they'll find us more beds tomorrow. I hope they find ones with better mattresses. I can't read because the only light is a wall light and it would disturb the others if I turned it on.

We arrived in the early evening. We've only been back in Berlin for a couple of days, and we thought we were going to stay in our bunker underneath the State Palace, but Papa suddenly came to fetch us this afternoon. He has decided that the best place for us to be is the Leader Bunker, or to be more precise, the Upper Bunker which leads to the Leader Bunker. It's much less comfortable than the bunker at home, no carpets, bare walls – at least in our bedroom – smaller beds, rougher sheets, thinner blankets.

Our Leader has come to the heart of Berlin to lead the final fight against the Russian hordes. We are here to show our support for him. Papa says we are very lucky to have this opportunity to demonstrate our loyalty. He says it is a very important moment in history and it is a great honour to take part in it. Our bravery is an example to all the German people. We are very close to victory, he says. Personally I don't think it really counts as being brave when you have no choice.

It's just the six of us and Papa and Mummy. We left both grannies and both governesses behind. When Papa phoned Swan Island to tell us to come to Berlin it was Hubi's day off and Miss Schroeter and Granny

Behrend had to help us pack, which was quite hard because Hubi's the only one who really knows where everything is. Mind you, we didn't need a lot. Papa had instructed that we should only bring one set of night things and one toy each as we are not going to be here long. We all brought our dolls – I brought Elsa – except of course Helmut, who brought a tank. Granny B. kept crying, and saying the same things over and over, "Tell your mother I must see her one more time. Give her a big kiss from me. I told her, I told her it would end in disaster. She should never have married him." It set us all off. Granny B. is always really rude about Papa. Mummy says it's because they don't see eye to eye. She says Granny B. is ridiculously melodramatic, and that the war will soon be won and we'll all be back together again. I don't know which house we'll live in after the war. I guess that it will take a while to clear up Berlin, so probably Swan Island would be best. Hopefully we will spend the whole summer there. I want to do lots of riding. I'm missing Rosamund already.

As soon as Hubi got back from her day off and heard that we'd left, she came to Berlin to find us. She arrived just as we were leaving the State Palace bunker. Helmut adores Hubi and burst out, without thinking as usual, "Are you coming with us to the Leader Bunker?", which was quite embarrassing because Mummy didn't say anything. She obviously didn't want Hubi to come. I suppose there's not enough room. Hubi looked at

15

Mummy and Mummy turned to us and said, "Come on, children, hurry up. Goodbye, Hubi." And Helmut called cheerily, "See you soon, Hubi!" as if we were off on a holiday.

We came to the bunker by car even though it's only a short walk from the State Palace. It's impossible to walk anywhere in Berlin nowadays. The pavements are covered with fallen bricks and broken glass. In some places a car can barely get down the middle of the road. And it was pouring with rain.

Mummy and Papa went ahead in the first car and us children in the second. I sat in the front. The driver was a funny-looking man with the squashed-in nose of a boxer and enormous ears. He wasn't one of the regular drivers. He annoyed me because he did that thing of talking to us in a way I just knew he wouldn't if our parents were there; trying to extract information he wouldn't dare ask them.

"I expect you're excited about going to the Leader Bunker."

"Oh yes!" said Helmut. "We're going to see Uncle Leader and there'll be lots of generals and soldiers. We'll be right in the thick of it."

"Will Miss Braun be there?"

I wasn't going to answer his questions. I am sure it is going to be secret exactly who is in the Leader Bunker. And Mummy is always telling us to be careful about what we say, especially to servants, but I think Helmut is still too young to understand why. He's nine and a half.

"Do you mean Auntie Eva?" Helmut asked solemnly. "Oh yes, I think she'll be there."

"Auntie Eva, eh!"

"She's not our real aunt," Helmut explained. "We just call her Auntie because she's a good friend of our family."

"You know her well, do you?"

"Quite well."

We've only met her a few times and we haven't seen her for ages – Helmut was just babbling now.

"I've heard she's very beautiful."

I don't think Helmut knew what to say to that.

Despite the rain, half the sky was glowing red from the Russian fires in the east. Heide thought it was the sunset and was clapping her hands because the sky looked so beautiful. She doesn't know east from west. Mummy tells them that the sound of the guns is thunder and yet they never seem to wonder why there are thunderstorms every day, even when it's sunny. I feel very alone.

We drove past one of the signs that Papa has had painted all over the city: "Every German will defend his capital. We shall stop the Red hordes at the walls of our Berlin." The driver didn't seem to be too worried about the Red hordes. "Ivan" he called them. "Ivan drinks so much vodka that he's more likely to shoot himself in the foot than to shoot a German soldier!" He laughed loudly to himself.

So many buildings have been shelled. Some have collapsed completely, and others are smashed open exposing flowery wallpaper and fireplaces and doors that lead nowhere. When we drove in from Swan Island the other day we saw mothers in overcoats cooking on open fires in the ruins and dirty barefoot children crouching around. I don't know what food they've got; there are hardly any shops still standing. We drove past one house which was on fire – huge yellow flames were billowing up out of the windows – and the houses either side standing solid as if nothing was happening. Helmut said he saw a dead body strung up on a lamp-post. He might have been lying.

We got out of the cars in the courtyard of the Empire Chancellery. It has been badly hit. There are huge holes in the roof of the building and the court-yard is heaped with rubble and burnt-out cars. All the glass in the windows has been broken, which gives the place the look of a skull. Papa says we shouldn't worry too much about all the damage because once we've won the war we will be able to rebuild the city bigger and better than ever before.

We went through a tall thin doorway at the back of the courtyard and down into the Empire Chancellery cellars. Inside there was no sign of damage at all. We went past the kitchens and into a large pantry, stacked with tinned fruit and jams and salamis and sausages and pickled beef and sacks of flour and sugar and crates and crates of wine and champagne. Then we went through a small door that looked like a cupboard, but was actually the entrance to a secret corridor. This led to a huge metal door guarded by soldiers with helmets and big, long guns. They searched our bags, even Mummy's handbag, before allowing us through. She wasn't at all pleased but the soldiers simply insisted it was "Leader's orders". Once we were allowed through, we started climbing down the stairs to the bunkers. There are hundreds of stairs – so many they make your legs go wobbly – and so many twists and turns of corridors that I lost all sense of direction. Hilde called it a labyrinth, but Mummy pointed out that luckily it leads to Uncle Leader, not the Minotaur. Helmut was very excited and kept saying, "Now we are in the middle of the total war!"

When we got down to the Leader Bunker, Papa went to find one of the secretaries to show us our room. Mummy's bedroom is next door to ours in the Upper Bunker but Papa's is down in the Leader Bunker so that he's always close to Uncle Leader. Mummy stayed downstairs to see Uncle Leader and then went straight to bed. She's got her bad heart again.

The secretary is called Mrs. Junge. You can tell she's not used to looking after children because she didn't make us brush our hair before bed and I think she would have even forgotten to get us to brush our teeth if I hadn't reminded her. She's kind though. As soon as we got here she said she was going to find things to "occupy us" and she took us down to the Leader Bunker and showed us a huge storeroom.

The room was full of the most unexpected things. It had been Uncle Leader's birthday a few days before and they had put all his presents in this room. Apparently he didn't want any of them and he'd told Mrs. Junge to let us pick out anything we fancied.

There were so many things – ornaments, toys, children's books – but none of it really suitable for a grown-up man.

"I want the teddy with the black nose!" Heide shouted, pointing at the top shelf. Mrs. Junge reached to get it down for her.

"Look! They've got Stukas Attack! Who'll play Stukas Attack with me?" Helmut asked, jumping up and down.

Deadly silence. Stukas Attack is the most boring board game in the world. None of us are ever going to want to play it with him.

"I will play Stukas Attack with you." said Mrs. Junge, passing the box to him. "Is there anything else you would like?"

"I'd love some of those tin soldiers, and…" Helmut had a good look around, "Could I take some cars as well? Mrs. Junge, why has Uncle Leader been given so many children's toys?"

"I have no idea. So many people love him and want to give him presents, but I think perhaps they don't know what to give him. What would the rest of you like?"

We picked up lots of paints, watercolour paper, playing cards and books. Hilde took some Red Indian stories, which Uncle Leader loves, and Holde took a great big book of the Grimm Brothers' *Children's and Household Tales* and a doll in traditional German costume.

We were just coming back up the big staircase, when the wail of the air raid siren started and immediately there was a massive explosion. Holde started to cry.

"There, there. Don't worry." Mrs. Junge crouched down beside her. "We are in the safest place in the city. No bomb can reach us down here."

Another explosion followed immediately. All the lights flickered, and bits of flaky ceiling fell down.

"You will soon get used to these bombs. I certainly have. We've been underground for nearly 100 days now. Come on, it's time for tea."

At least she admits that there are bombs. I'm hoping I might be able to get some truth out of her.

Cheese and salami sandwiches, chocolate cake and hot chocolate were all laid out on a big table in the corridor. Miss Manziarly served us. She's Uncle Leader's special cook. The only person he trusts to cook for him.

She's Austrian and has a very strong accent, a bun of dark hair, a tight apron and thick fingers. She said that Uncle Leader had insisted that she make us chocolate cake. She cut us six very fair and even slices. Holde didn't want any chocolate cake because she doesn't really eat anything except bread and butter, but Miss Manziarly didn't make a fuss about that. She said she was used to people being particular. Uncle Leader eats chocolate cake every day and never eats meat.

After tea Auntie Eva came to see us. She gave us each a kiss. She puts her cheek against your cheek and she has the softest skin in the world and she just kisses the air beside your ear, and you get this lovely waft of cologne. She looks like she's in a movie. Her hair curls back in flicks around her face. Her eyebrows are plucked so neatly they look like they have been painted on. Or maybe they have been. Her lips make a perfect red love heart. And her finger nails are all exactly the same length, curved into identical points and matching the colour of her lipstick. She looks incredibly clean. I don't know how you get that clean. Especially not here. Anyway, she had fantastic news, which is that Uncle Adi's – she calls him Uncle Adi – Alsatian, Blondi, has had puppies! We all followed her swish-swish dress down to the Leader Bunker to see them.

The puppies are gorgeous! They're really tiny; it's hard to believe that they're going to grow into great big dogs like Blondi. They're only two weeks old, and brown and golden and covered in messy fluffy hair, really soft! There are five of them, two girls and three boys: Foxl (my favourite, she's named after a terrier that Uncle Adi had during the First World War); Stasi (which was the name of one of Auntie Eva's favourite old dogs); Wolf (Auntie Eva says he's Uncle Adi's favourite); Harass (he's named after their father); and Luger (Auntie Eva says he's named after a person who inspired Uncle Adi, not the gun). Auntie Eva said we could have one to take home after the war. We couldn't agree which one. I really wanted Foxl because she fell asleep on my lap, but Helmut really wanted Luger because he's the biggest. In the end Auntie Eva said that we could ask Mummy if we could have two dogs.

Auntie Eva sat at her little desk and wrote a letter. All her things are beautiful. Thick cream paper, and a smart black fountain pen. She makes you forget that you're under the ground in the middle of a war. After a bit she went to call Mrs. Junge to take us back to bed. Auntie Eva says we can play hide-and-seek down in the Leader Bunker tomorrow.

"And don't be afraid of the soldiers," she said. "Everyone is so pleased you're here!"

It was pouring with rain the day we first visited the house on Swan Island. We sheltered on the wide veranda whilst Papa opened the front door with a giant key. Inside it was pitch dark. He went round opening all the tall wooden shutters, letting in a dull green light from the dripping overgrown garden. I pretended I was a mermaid in an underwater palace.

I loved the large echoey rooms, the cupboards you could hide in, the bedrooms with faded flowery wallpaper. We explored everywhere – the kitchens, the cellars, the bathrooms with their vast stained baths. There was so much to see that Mummy had a touch of her heart trouble and had to stop to catch her breath in one of the servants' rooms in the attic. She sat down on an old iron bed that the people before had left behind, and I climbed on her lap and we just sat quietly listening to Papa whooping with delight downstairs and she smiled a secret Papa-is-mad-but-we-don't-mind smile at me, and I remember the soft dip of her shoulder where my head fitted just right and feeling that everything was going to be perfect from then on. I didn't realise that when we actually moved in the whole house would be freshly painted and done up and all the beauty and mystery would be decorated away.

Luckily the garden took longer for them to sort out. It was enormous and had been what Mummy called "neglected". There were thick bushes and low branches and secret places where only children could fit. In the end they got a man called Carl with fierce, blue eyes and a mower and a scythe and he pretty well ruined everything, but for a while it hid whole other worlds to play in.

That first visit, after the rain stopped, the long grass was still drenched, and we walked right down to the edge of the lake, my socks and shoes soaked through. There was a girl in the garden next door, swinging on a swing, gum-booted feet in the sky. She waved, but Mummy told us not to wave back. She said that, unfortunately, the one problem with the house was that the neighbours were unsuitable. She said Papa would sort it out.

I hated Carl the cutter but I loved Mr. Bruegger who looked after the ponies. Papa bought two ponies – Loki and Freya, both piebald – and a pony trap. Mr. Bruegger would take us out in the trap for rides around the island, and afterwards he would let us feed the ponies. Mr. Bruegger taught us how to ride and how to whistle and how to touch stinging nettles without getting stung and he used to tell us stories about the horses he had looked after during the war. I loved the ponies. I loved their warm breath and soft noses and the smell of hay in their stable. It was only later that we got Rosamund for me to ride.

In those early days, before the war, we used to have

to go sailing on *Baldur*, Papa's yacht. There was always a cold breeze on the lake and we had to wear damp, heavy life jackets. I always got told off for being in the wrong place: "Mind the boom!"

Papa had a friend called Lida who was a film star. Sometimes Papa and I used to watch her films but Mummy didn't like them and Hilde and Helmut were too young. Lida was very beautiful. Well, Mummy didn't think so, but I did. She had lovely wavy hair and her face was somehow tight and bright and always smiling. Lida loved going out in Papa's yacht and Mummy would always make me and Hilde go too to keep her company because she thought Lida would get bored with only Papa to talk to. I don't think it was true because Papa and Lida would always go off for one more sail after they dropped us back home.

❧

It was the first summer at Swan Island that I met Reggie.

We were always sent out to play in the garden after breakfast and sometimes I would go off on my own to see if I could catch a glimpse of the girl next door. The fence running round the edge of the garden had collapsed so it was hard to tell where our garden stopped and the neighbour's began. This was before Carl put up the new fence with barbed wire. One day I was sitting, hidden, or so I thought, in the bushes, watching her doing handstands, when she suddenly sprang through to our side, and flung herself down beside me.

"Let me introduce myself. I am Regine Goldschmidt. Queen of the Goldschmidts. Who, pray, are you?"

"My name's Helga." I didn't know what to say next because Mummy had banned us from talking to the neighbours, so I spoke very quietly as a compromise between the "Don't talk to the neighbours" and the "Speak when you're spoken to" rules.

"I'm afraid I'm not allowed to talk to you," I said in a whisper.

"How ridiculous! It's probably because we're Jewish. But you needn't worry – it's not catching!"

"Are you allowed to talk to us?"

"I'm allowed to do whatever I want. I haven't got a mother." She twisted a long strand of dark hair around her finger.

"Have you got a papa?"

"Oh yes. And a brother and a sister, but they are grown up, pretty well, and they only come at weekends. So it's just me and Father here and deadly boring. I can't wait till the holidays are over and I go back to school in Berlin. You can call me Reggie by the way."

"What happened to your mother?"

"She died."

"Why?"

"She was struck by lightning."

"Here?"

27

"No, of course not. She wasn't really. She had an illness."

"How old are you?"

"I'm twelve and a half. Is it true that your father is Josef Goebbels?"

"Yes. Why?"

"Do you know Adolf Hitler?"

"Do you mean the Leader?"

"Some people call him that."

"We call him Uncle Leader."

"Is he your uncle?"

"Not my real uncle."

"Is he scary?"

"No, he's not really scary, but he's smelly."

"My father says he's a very dangerous man. How many brothers and sisters do you have?"

"Two sisters and two brothers. I'm the oldest – except for Harald, he's sixteen, but he's only my half-brother and he mostly lives with his father – Hilde is three and a half, Helmut is nearly two and Holde is just a baby."

"Is that all? Father always says Goebbels has hundreds of children – at least 23 or something."

"Oh bother, that's Cook calling. I've got to go to lunch. Be here the same time tomorrow!"

After that I used to look for Regine, Queen of the Goldschmidts, whenever I could. She would come over to our side and we would lie in the grass and she would tell me stories about her school, and show me how to do the splits, which I never could. I remember one lovely warm day, she took me over to her side, down to a jetty sticking out into the lake at the bottom of their garden, and we sat dangling our feet and making little ripples in the still, still water. No one saw us.

After that the days became cooler and I had to wear a cardigan. I looked for Regine in the usual place, after breakfast and after lunch, but she wasn't there any more. She must have gone back to Berlin.

❦

Uncle Leader used to come and stay a lot – Mummy did up a special guest house for him so that he could come whenever he wanted. He came for my fifth birthday and he gave me a toy sewing machine. Even though it was a toy, it really worked. It was beautiful: shiny black metal decorated with gold flowers. I immediately pictured all the gorgeous dresses I was going to be able to make.

"How does it work?"

"I'm afraid I've no idea – your mother will have to show you."

Mummy sent for an old sheet.

I didn't want a dress made out of an old sheet.

"I'll show you how to hem."

I didn't want to know how to hem.

"We'll start with a handkerchief!"

Mummy cut a small square.

She leant over me and directed my hands to push the material into place. Her big ring squashed into my fingers.

"No, no, no... Helga, hold it flat. I'll do the pedal."

I DON'T WANT TO MAKE A STUPID HANDKERCHIEF! I thought, but I didn't say. I held my tongue. The stitches rushed along: one, two, three, four sides, closed neatly over.

"There," Mummy said. "Lovely. All done. Show Uncle Leader what a clever girl you are."

<hr />

Papa had his own guest house too and he used to stay there so that he could work undisturbed. Mummy said we made too much noise for him to concentrate, but I think she did more shouting than we did. Lida must have been good at keeping quiet because she was allowed.

Day Two in the Bunker
Monday 23 April, 1945

I was the last one to wake up this morning. I can vaguely remember Helmut turning on the light at some point, but I just pulled the blanket over my eyes and fell back to sleep. When I woke up properly Helmut was firing elastic bands at the door handle; Hilde was reading a book about the Red Indians and Holde and Hedda and Heide had "gone to Iceland", which is what they call it when they dive down under the sheets to the bottom of the bed and pretend it's an igloo.

Mrs. Junge came to call us for breakfast. She looked like she'd got up in a hurry. Her hair was flat on one side and sticking up on the other. She told us that Mummy was having a lie-in because her heart was still bad.

We had hot chocolate and bread and butter and

damson jam for breakfast. You can pretty well have as much butter as you like, which is so nice – the first time in ages that we haven't had to scrape it really thin to try and make the ration last as long as possible – and the bread was still warm so the butter melted. One of the kitchen orderlies had just collected it from a bakery off William Street. Miss Manziarly says that the kitchen orderlies are braver than half the bunker soldiers. She thinks it is probably the only bakery left in Berlin.

Papa came to see us after breakfast. He told us that the astrologers predict that we will win the war by the end of April. That's only a week away. Apparently the stars are almost exactly the same as when Frederick the Great won the Seven Year War by a miracle. That time the Empress of Russia died, and this time the American President has just died. Which has got to be more than a coincidence, Papa says. Papa always used to say that only silly old fools like Mr. Goering believed in astrology, but now everyone seems to believe it. I hope it's true. I couldn't bear the thought of being cooped up down here for more than a week. When we get back to Swan Island the first thing I'm going to do is cartwheel all the way around the lawn. I can't wait till it's warm enough to go swimming – there's probably only a month to go. Hubi's going to teach me butterfly this summer.

Mummy stayed in bed all morning. At lunchtime she came and sat with us as we ate our sandwiches but she didn't eat anything. She looked very white and tired. One really good thing is that all the little ones know not to bicker if Mummy's poorly. She told us that after lunch we would have a rest and then she would come and help us get ready for tea with Uncle Leader. A rest! As if there is anything to rest from. All that exhausting drawing and reading. Mummy kissed our heads and went back to her room.

Just before lunch we had a game of hide-and-seek. I was the counter and the others hid. Heide and Hedda were quite easy to find because they had gone back to their igloo, which I guessed. All the others were hiding down in the washrooms in the Leader Bunker where Blondi and the puppies live. They were easy to find too because the puppies were barking like mad in their little high-pitched voices. Papa was in the Leader Bunker corridor, but he had his concentrating face on, so I didn't say hello. There's a tall man, Mr. Misch, who is the telephone operator. He came out of his little booth and whispered in my ear, "Best to go back upstairs, those little ones are a making a bit of a racket." So I gathered them all up and found Miss Manziarly in the upper dining-room corridor setting out our sandwiches.

Some orderlies had put an extra bunk in our room during the morning. When we went for our supposed rest Hedda and Heide and Helmut immediately started squabbling about who should have the top bunk. They gave me a headache. In the end I read them the story of Hansel and Gretl just to get them to be quiet.

Eventually Mummy and Auntie Eva and Auntie Eva's maid Liesl came in to get us ready for tea. I like the look of Liesl. She's sort of cosy and up-together and smells of ironing. She's one of those people who gives you the feeling that they could cope with anything, without making a fuss. Mummy had put her face on so she looked a bit brighter. Auntie Eva was wearing another swishy dress – covered in red roses. Mummy seemed in a bit of a dream. Auntie Eva was nattering away about how impossible it has been to find good quality dressmakers now all the Jews have left Berlin and Mummy was just nodding as she got out our best clothes – the white dresses, and Helmut's white shirt and shorts – and gave them to Liesl to press. I'm so glad we didn't bring those ones she had made out of the nursery curtains – they're horribly stiff and make us look like lampshades.

Once we were all ready we had a quick run-through of our songs: the one about the nightingale and "Little Stars". They were OK. Auntie Eva clapped loudly – which sounded so hollow as it echoed around the concrete room – and said we were wonderful little darlings, and that Uncle Adi would love our performance. We are just what he needs to get him through this difficult time. Heide shouts more than she sings but it won't matter because everyone always thinks she's sweet.

Normally we would give Uncle Adi flowers for his birthday but obviously we can't get any flowers down here, so we just took cards we'd made him. Mine is of edelweiss. Hedda is going to recite the poem she learnt for Christmas.

Uncle Adi's sitting room was quite crowded with all of us in it. Papa and Mrs. Junge were already there, sitting on the only two chairs. They both jumped up to offer their chairs to Mummy and Auntie Eva. There was also a small flowery sofa, but they seemed to prefer to lean against the desk, rather than sit there. We children sat on the floor, tucking our legs under us to take up as little room as possible and we waited while Auntie Eva fetched Uncle Adi.

My first thought when I saw him was that he had shrunk. He was stooped forward and looked crumpled, like he needed Liesl to give him a good iron. As he came in we all jumped up, but not quick enough for Mummy who gave me a little poke in the back, which really annoyed me because I'm old enough, for goodness' sake, to remember my manners without being reminded. I curtsied and shook his hand. Horrible, moist and limp; that hadn't changed. Hilde came next, but when it came to Helmut's turn, Uncle Leader grabbed him by one of his ears and gave it a shake which went on embarrassingly long until Helmut's ear was bright red. I could see Helmut was holding his breath in order to stifle a yelp. Finally Uncle Leader let go and dropped down on to the sofa with a fart. It could have been the sofa squeaking, but I think it was a fart. Auntie Eva sat down beside him.

"What a delight to see such beautiful children!"

"The children are very happy to be here, my Leader," said Papa. "They are very excited to join you in your underground cave."

"Our cave! Oh yes, it is wonderful to be in a cave… a grotto!" said Auntie Eva. "It is a great adventure." And her eyes blazed as if she had never wanted anything in her whole life more than to be here.

"The children have cards for you, My Leader," said Mummy. "They have made them themselves, even little Heide. Children, give Uncle Adi your cards."

Uncle Adi examined each card in turn. "My favourite presents are pictures painted by children. Girls and boys. Some people say that women cannot paint, but Angelica Kauffmann was a great painter, and painting makes a good hobby for a woman." I've no idea who Angelica Kauffmann is. At this point he farted really loudly and it was definitely him, even though everyone pretended they hadn't noticed. I could see Helmut was about to get the giggles so I gave him a sharp nudge.

"The children also have a song for you, my Leader." Mummy went on, "They have been practising especially for your birthday."

"Wonderful! Let's hear it." We all squashed into our places and Mummy stood in front of us to conduct.

Night silence everywhere
Only by the stream
The nightingale
Sings her sad song
Softly through the valley

It was a bit squeaky, certainly not as soft as the nightingale, but not too bad. Uncle Adi clapped one hand on his thigh, which seemed to be slightly shaking all the time. He was clinging on to the bottom of his jacket with his other hand.

"Wonderful! Wonderful! Can you sing me another?"

Our second song – "Can you count the stars?" – was much longer, ending with the verse:

Do you know how many children
Rise each morning blithe and gay?
Can you count their jolly voices,
Singing sweetly day by day?
God hears all the happy voices,
In their merry songs rejoices;
And He loves them, every one
And He loves them, every one

Uncle Adi clapped his thigh enthusiastically. I thought he was appreciating our singing but then I saw that Miss Manziarly had appeared in the doorway carrying a huge tray of cakes and behind her was one of the kitchen orderlies with a big jug of hot chocolate and a pot of tea.

"Is there chocolate cake for the children? They deserve a reward for their wonderful singing!"

I have never seen anyone eat cake as fast as Uncle Adi. He kept cramming it into his mouth, showering his lap with crumbs. Watching Uncle Adi, Heide just grabbed a second piece of chocolate cake from the plate and stuffed it straight into her mouth. I thought Papa would pick her up and take her out, but he just bent down and whispered something in her ear. Heide stared down at the floor and I could tell that she was trying to swallow her mouthful without moving her face, because she had to keep it completely still to stop herself crying.

Suddenly Helmut jumped up, almost knocking over his hot chocolate.

"U-U-Uncle Leader, I have written a special speech for you for your birthday." He pulled a piece of paper from his shorts' pocket:

"The Leader is the man of the century. He is sure of himself despite pain and suffering. He shows us the way to victory. He will not sell his faith or his ideals. He always and without doubt follows the straight path to his goal!"

I couldn't believe Helmut was pretending that he had written these words. We had all listened on the radio to Papa giving his birthday speech for Uncle Leader just a few days ago.

"Helmut, don't lie! You stole that from Papa!" I

couldn't let him get away with it.

All the grown-ups laughed, which I wasn't expecting, but they laughed even louder when Helmut replied:

"No, Papa stole it from me!"

Then Papa suggested that Hedda recite her poem:

It has to get light again,
After these dark days,
Let us not ask if we will see it.
New light will rise again.

She said it really quietly. There was a hesitation and then everyone clapped. For a second I thought Auntie Eva was going to cry but she jumped to her feet:

"I know! Let's fetch the little sausages!" I thought she meant more food but she meant the puppies. Me and Hilde and Helmut went with her. I carried Foxl and Wolf and then gave Wolf to Uncle Adi, and kept Foxl to cuddle myself.

"Now, children, it's my Blondi's turn to sing!" said Uncle Adi.

He started her off by giving a long howl – like a wolf. Heide grabbed my hand. Blondi joined in with a very high-pitched howl.

Then Uncle Adi made a much softer, deep, low howl, more like a groan, and Blondi copied. Heide held my hand even tighter. Everyone else laughed.

"Good girl, Blondi, good girl." Uncle Adi held up

three fingers and Blondi stopped howling, and immediately sat and wagged her tail along the floor, and Uncle Adi rewarded her with three little pieces of cake. Not the chocolate one – he says chocolate is bad for dogs – but a sponge cake. And then we gave the puppies a tiny piece each.

"You see I'm really Dr. Doolittle, I can talk to the animals. Have you ever seen Blondi do a schoolgirl?"

"No, show us, show us!" Heide burst out. I think she was so relieved that the wolf bit was over. So Uncle Leader tapped the arm of the couch and Blondi lifted up her front legs and hung them over the side of the arm and looked at him with her head on one side, and her face looked completely, completely obedient.

"She's a good schoolgirl," said Uncle Adi, patting her on the head. "Like you, Helga. I'm sure you're a good schoolgirl. What have you been learning at school?"

I wasn't sure what to say, because we haven't been able to go to school for ages, but I didn't say that because I didn't want to remind him of the war and everything, so I just tried to think of something we'd been doing when I was last at school.

"We have been studying Geography, Uncle Leader."

"Well, what have they taught you?"

"That the German Empire used to be much bigger, but the land was stolen from us by Poland and Russia after the Great War, and now we are recapturing that land so that there is sufficient living space for every

German." As I said it I realised that it was the most tactless thing I could have said, because the Russians are taking over that land right now, but I didn't know how to stop once I'd started. Luckily Uncle Leader didn't seem to mind.

"Very good, my Helga, very good. And do you like your teachers?"

"Yes, Uncle Leader." I don't particularly, especially since the war started and they've brought all the old ones out of retirement, but I thought that was the best thing to say.

"Well, you are a very lucky girl. My school teachers were terrible. I hated them. Everything I learnt I taught myself. I have very rarely met a school teacher who is not an idiot. Some of them were Jews, of course, in my day. At least you haven't had to suffer that. At Steyr we had a Jewish teacher, a science teacher. We locked him in his laboratory. How he howled! Almost as good as Blondi! He had no authority over us, none at all. We had no respect for him…"

Uncle Adi seemed to drift off into his memories and Mummy ushered us quietly out. Auntie Eva stayed sitting on the sofa beside him, wearing her pretty smile.

The corridor of the Upper Bunker is full of soldiers. One of them looks only a year or two older than me. I've only seen him hurrying through, but he's got a nice face. Some are guarding the doorways but most of them are just sitting around. They all smoke, which is quite surprising as Uncle Leader hates smoking and he never used to allow anyone to smoke near him. When we were staying in the Berghof, Mummy always used to have to slip outside without Uncle Leader noticing because it made him so angry if anyone smoked, even in the gardens. I suppose he's got more important things to worry about now. Anyway, it means that the corridors really smell of smoke, and it makes your clothes smell. Not that that's the worst smell here. Most of the soldiers have a disgusting, beery, old-man smell.

It's odd because I always think of soldiers as being very smart – even the ones we saw when we visited the military hospital, who were missing parts of their body, still had smart uniforms. I always used to picture typical soldiers with shiny buttons and shiny boots, shiny medals and shiny faces. At Castle Lanke, Head Storm Leader Schwagermann was forever polishing his boots and polishing his buttons. But today he came to see us and he was all dusty, he had buttons missing and he hadn't even shaved. Not that that bothered Hedda. She wants to marry him because she loves his glass eye. She thinks it's fantastic that he can pop it in and out.

One exception to the general shabbiness is Upper Group Leader Fegelein, or Uncle Hermann, as Auntie Eva introduced him to us in the corridor. He's married to her sister Gretl, which doesn't exactly make him an uncle of ours. He is impeccably smart. Every hair oiled into place, all shiny parts polished, a strong whiff of cologne. He showed us his pistol, which is gold with a mother-of-pearl handle, more like jewellery than a weapon. I didn't like the look of him to be honest. He's got one of those chins that slides backwards and a great big moon of a forehead. Gretl is expecting their baby any day.

At bedtime I quietly asked Mrs. Junge if she had any news of the fighting. She didn't. I asked her how long she thought we'd be here. She said she had no idea. She stroked my hair, and she looked so sad that I knew there had to be something she wasn't telling me.

I keep getting this knot in my stomach – and a feeling of being stifled. There's a heaviness in the air, and not just because it is stuffy down here – there's a heaviness hanging over everyone. I could feel it at teatime; behind the jolly talk there's a dull tiredness. Mrs. Junge shows it most, and Liesl. They don't hide the bags under their eyes with face powder and rouge like Auntie Eva and Mummy.

I've been lying in the dark for ages now. It's quieter in the corridor tonight. I can hear some singing and laughing – I think it's the soldiers – but fewer footsteps tramping past than last night.

Tonight I want to dream about Horst Caspar, to imagine him coming to rescue us, just like he does in the film *Kohlberg*. He will have found a secret tunnel which leads right out of Berlin. I'll be the last to go down it. He will take me by the hand and we'll run

down the tunnel together and out into the bright sun-
light.

We are having breakfast at Swan Island. Papa is sitting at the head of the table opening letters. Suddenly he whoops with delight and claps his hands.

"At last! The old Jew's finally given in. I knew our friends in the police would get him to see sense. It's going to be fantastic. We'll have the largest property on Swan Island. The garden will be twice the size it is now. We will have more guest houses, games rooms, a proper cinema."

"What?"

Mummy corrects me: "Don't say 'what', Helga, it isn't nice."

"Excuse me, Papa, what do you mean?"

"I've bought the house next door. And for a song. The old Jew tried to diddle us at first, but he's come round."

"Next door?"

"What's the matter with you, Helga? Your brain doesn't seem to be working this morning. Perhaps you swapped brains with Helmut during the night? Yes, next door."

"What's going to happen to the people who live there now?" I try hard not to let my voice tremble.

"Who cares? They're going to live in France, or something. Somewhere a long way away. They were a bad lot. They should never have been allowed to live here.

All their money had been stolen from the German people. They were lucky to get a *pfennig* for the place. Swan Island is going to be completely clear of Jews. The Speers have snapped up the Goldschmidt-Rothschild place. So you'll soon have plenty of playmates. Did I mention, sweetie, Albert and Margret Speer are visiting their new acquisition this afternoon and I've invited them to drop by for tea? I've no idea whether they're bringing the children."

I can't finish my breakfast. I carefully drop my sausage under the table so that Blitz, our puppy, can gobble it. I have to find Reggie.

"Mummy, please can I get down?"

"Yes, if you've finished, Helga."

"Can I go and feed the chickens?"

"Yes. Go and collect the scraps from Cook, and take Hilde with you."

As soon as we're outside I grab Hilde by the hand, swear her to secrecy – she's not very trustworthy but I have to risk it – and together we run down to the bushes where I usually meet Reggie. We lie down in the grass and wait. It is damp and soon the grass begins to itch my skin. Hilde starts to whimper because of the cold. My tummy begins to rumble, but still there is no sign of Reggie, or anyone. We walk back to the house. Papa is on the steps.

"Where have you been?"

"Feeding the chickens."

"You are a liar, Helga Goebbels. You have not been feeding the chickens. You have not been anywhere near the chickens. Have you any idea of the anxiety you have caused your mother? Where have you been?"

"In the garden, Papa. Sorry, Papa."

"Hilde. Stop that noise. Go to the nursery. Helga, you come with me!"

He leads me into the drawing room.

"Take off your coat."

He sits down.

"Take off your pants."

"Come here and bend over my knee."

"Five smacks for a five-year-old liar. If you ever lie to me or your mother again you will get twice that number. Now go to the bathroom and wash your face. The Speers will soon be here for tea. You don't want them to see you've been a cry-baby."

<hr />

I never saw Reggie again. Papa moved into her house. He called it his citadel. Mummy wouldn't let him in our house any more. He telephoned, but she wouldn't let us speak to him. When I had the chance, I would go and look for him in the spot where I used to look for Reggie, but he was never there.

State Secretary Hanke from Papa's office came every day to help Mummy with everything. She called him her rock. They went riding together. Cook would make them a picnic and they'd be gone all day.

Papa telephoned on my birthday. Mummy said I could talk to him for a minute. He was crying on the phone, "Please tell Mummy to let me come back. Tell her everything can be sorted out."

I plucked up the courage to talk to her about it the next day, but it didn't do any good. She gave me one of her you-should-know-better looks: "I'm afraid your Papa has been too naughty to be allowed home."

I didn't ask again, but suddenly one wet afternoon she told us to get our coats on because Nanny – I can't actually remember which nanny it was, I can just remember her dark gabardine raincoat and her revolting handkerchief – was going to take me and Hilde and Helmut to visit him in the citadel. We were allowed half an hour.

We were so excited that as soon as we got there we all jumped on top of him and fell down together on to the sofa, still wearing our gumboots and raincoats. I'd forgotten how much I missed him, and also how bony he was. I whispered in his ear, so that the others couldn't hear, telling him how he had to say a big sorry to Mummy and promise to be good. He smelled lovely and Papa-like. Half an hour was gone in a flash and Nanny came to the door to take us home. We didn't want to go. Hilde started crying and that set us all off, including Papa. His nose went bright red and started dripping. He couldn't find a handkerchief in his pocket, so Nanny whipped one out and he had a good blow before giving it back to her. When we got to the front steps of the main house, Nanny took it out again to wipe our wet faces.

I made up my mind never to be naughty again.

~❦~

One thing that always brings Mummy and Papa back together again is an invitation from Uncle Leader. Like cigarettes, arguments are banned in the Leader's presence. Especially arguments between married couples. Uncle Leader is completely against divorce. Mummy says that is because he has never been married. She says that people who haven't been married don't understand how difficult it is. She divorced Harald's father because she got married too young and she didn't know what she was doing. She says that she and Papa will never get divorced, but they just have to live apart sometimes when things are difficult. Papa has a bedroom next to his office in Berlin so that he can stay there when things are difficult. One night, after he'd been staying in his office for quite a while, he came home after work to pick up Mummy and Hilde and me, to take us to a party for Uncle Leader. Hilde and I were very excited because we hadn't seen Papa for ages but also because we were being allowed to stay up late to watch a torchlight procession. Hilde and I sat on Mummy's bed and watched her get ready. She looked so beautiful – like a mermaid in a long shimmery dress, her hair making little waves around her face. I helped her do up the clasp on her necklace and she pinned a cascade of silk flowers to the front of her dress. Papa clapped his hands when he saw her, and I don't think she stopped smiling all evening.

We all gathered on the upstairs balconies to watch the procession. Children at the front. It was a really dark night. We could hear the band before we could see anything. We craned our necks to see the first torches. It was like a river of stars flowing into the street beneath us – as if we were looking down on the sky. The stars flowed on and on until they reached as far as the eye could see in both directions. Uncle Leader took my hand. "My favourite little German girl," he said and squeezed it tightly. I felt so proud. He prefers me to Hilde!

Suddenly there was a huge bang and a great spray of fireworks lit up the sky. Silver, gold, red, green. Everyone cheered. Uncle Leader bent down to whisper to Papa. I remember Papa silencing the room with a shout, in order to call a toast for Mr. Speer who had designed the fireworks. His words echoed around the room and Mr. Speer bowed his head and smiled at the floor. Then the band started playing "Germany, Germany Above All" and we all sang at the tops of our voices. We are the greatest country in the world! Uncle Leader is laughing. Everyone is happy. Mummy and

Papa are standing together and smiling brightly, their faces pink with happiness.

I can remember marching up the stairs to bed that night, pretending I was carrying my own flaming torch, determined to keep it alight inside me for ever. Papa came back with us and stayed that night.

Day Three in the Bunker
Tuesday 24 April, 1945

I woke up in the middle of the night. Very suddenly. I don't know what woke me. It was quiet except for the sleepy breathing sounds of the little ones and the hum of the ventilation. No footsteps or bombs or guns. It was as if I'd had a nightmare, but I couldn't remember what it was. Just a black emptiness. I didn't dare sit up. I wanted to call out for Mummy but I didn't want to make a sound in case there were Russians who'd broken into the bunker and were waiting silently to pounce. I lay completely still so that no one would know I was there, trying to breathe tiny silent breaths through my nose without moving my chest. I thought I could hear someone outside our door. I tilted my head to see if I could see any shadows in the strip of light under the door but there was nothing there.

I must have fallen back to sleep in the end because

the next thing I remember was being woken by a thudding explosion. Bits of plaster fell on my face. We turned on the light but no one came. It was 7.30, so we got dressed in silence, not even Helmut saying a word, and waited for Mrs. Junge to come and get us for breakfast.

Everything always looks the same here whether it's the middle of the day or the middle of the night, so what if the clock was completely wrong and we didn't know? It could have been 10.30 in the morning and no one had come to get us because everyone had been killed in the night. I got the tight feeling again – of a large pebble under my ribs, which stops my breath going any further down than the bottom of my neck. But I didn't let on to the little ones.

I felt a bit better once Mrs. Junge had finally come for us and we'd had some breakfast. We took our books and paints out to the landing table, and the little ones brought teddies and Helmut brought his soldiers and cars. I tried to do a painting – a washy blue sky – but all this playing and doing things just seems pointless. The same question keeps going round and round my head, the question no one will answer and no one will talk about: WHAT'S GOING TO HAPPEN TO US? I told Mrs. Junge that I had a headache and I went back to our bedroom on my own and screamed into the pillow.

I was lying there holding Elsa really tight – her old

face always looks so sad and comforting; she has tiny tiny cracks around her eyes and mouth, which make her, I think, much more beautiful than brand-new dolls – when Liesl came to collect our dirty clothes for washing. She scooped everything up into her basket and I thought maybe she hadn't noticed me all scrunched up on the bed, but then she came and stood beside me and rubbed my back.

"Chin up!" she said.

I've heard the soldiers say that, although they add: "while you've still got a chin!"

"I expect you need a hug."

I climbed down on to the lower bunk, and we both sat down with our heads resting on each other because there wasn't enough height to sit upright. Liesl felt warm and soft.

"There, there. Don't take on. We're all going to look after each other. Where there's life there's hope."

I didn't mean to cry but I couldn't help it. Liesl had a clean hanky, which she passed to me. The feeling of her warmth beside me gave me a bit of courage.

"Liesl, what do you think will happen if we lose the war?"

"Don't be silly. We won't lose the war. Give your face a good wipe."

"But what if we did? Don't you ever worry that we might?"

She paused. "Of course I do. It's only natural to

worry, but you have to keep hoping or you'll go mad."

"What do you want to do when we get out of here?"

"I want to go home. I want to see my parents. I want to sleep in my own bed. I want to open my curtains in the morning and look out at the farmyard. I want to hear the cockerel crow, I want to hear the dogs bark, I want to drink warm milk, fresh from the cow, and I want to see Peter."

She spoke softly and dreamily, but the last few words came out in a strange, twisted voice. I could see her tears. I didn't know what to do, so I just rubbed the back of her hand until her sobs died down, and she let go of me for a moment and wiped her face quickly. She doesn't have to worry about smudging like Mummy. If Mummy cries she always presses under each eye with a straight finger, trying to stop her eye make-up running down her cheeks.

"Who's Peter?"

"Peter is my fiancé."

"Is he a farmer?"

"No, no, no. Peter is a bookseller. Well, he works for his father who has a bookshop. He lives in a little town about two miles from my parents' farm. But he's in the army at the moment."

"Is he here in Berlin?" I didn't mean to set her off crying again.

"No, I'm not sure where he is exactly. It's difficult with Auntie Eva. We have to move about a lot. Our whereabouts are secret. Letters don't always get through. I haven't heard from him for, well, for a long time. He was sent to the Eastern Front."

"Do you have a picture of him?"

She did. Tucked in a pocket of her chemise, so it was a bit warm and crumpled. Not in uniform, but dressed in a suit. A serious face. Dark hair parted on the side and flopping down over one eye. He looked clever and certain and very far away.

"He's very handsome," I said.

Liesl nodded and shifted herself upright. "I must get on. This washing won't do itself. But I feel better for a cry. Thank you, Helga. Please don't tell Auntie Eva I got upset. She likes everyone to keep cheerful. Let's go and see what the others are up to."

We went back to the round table where Mrs. Junge had got the others playing a game of forfeits. Papa and Mummy ate lunch with us. Well, Papa ate. Mummy wasn't hungry. We had thin, pale brown soup and mashed potato. A bit of an odd combination. Mash is another Uncle Adi favourite, apparently. Actually, I'm not surprised because Miss Manziarly makes excellent mash. No lumps. Even Holde ate a bit. Tinned peaches for pudding. Not a patch, mind, on the peaches in the greenhouse on Swan Island.

We were just about to go for our afternoon rest when Auntie Eva came running up the staircase: "Darlings! Would you like to come and have a bath? Uncle Adi is in a meeting, so we won't be in his way. You can all have a bath in our bathroom! Helga, darling, can you help everyone find their towels?"

Auntie Eva and Uncle Adi have the only bath in the bunker, and usually nobody except them is allowed to use it. It's not exactly luxurious. Stone floor, concrete walls, just the single bare bulb dangling from the middle of the ceiling. And it smells pretty bad. A mixture of diesel and damp, I think. Not the kind of bathroom you'd expect Auntie Eva to have, although she has, of course, made the most of it. There's a candle, and a shelf full of her perfumes and powders and bath salts. And her beautiful lace dressing gown hanging on the door. When we went in she gave the room a quick spray of cologne. The tap water came out rather slowly and rather brown, but she threw in handfuls of bath salts which disguised the colour a bit. The main thing was that the water was so deliciously hot.

"OK, children. You are going to need to squeeze up really tight."

My face must have fallen because Auntie Eva gave me a look and quickly changed her mind.

"Actually, no, Helga can have the water first, then Holde and Hilde can share, then Hedda and Heide, and last of all Helmut can have the bath to himself."

It was just bliss to sink down into the deep warm water, and drift away from everything – all the dirt and the rubble and the smelly soldiers. I closed my eyes and plunged my head down under the water. Heaven. But brief heaven, because I knew all the others were waiting and wanting the water while it was still hot. Auntie Eva had warmed the towels on the hot pipes for us, and I sat wrapped up in one in her room for a little while, simply enjoying being warm. Most of the time I feel just slightly chilly. Auntie Eva says the bunker is kept cool because Uncle Leader hates being hot. Apparently he can think better when he's cold. I'm the opposite.

Liesl had clean clothes ready for us, and I got dressed while Auntie Eva was what she calls "repairing" her make-up. Liesl dried and combed my hair, very gently, and then I had a cuddle with Foxl.

After everyone had had their baths and got dressed, it was time for tea with Uncle Adi. We went through to his sitting room with the dogs. He was already there, sitting on the sofa, and he patted his lap for Heide to jump on to it.

"Here, sing me a nice song, Heide." It's amazing how she isn't shy. Immediately she started bouncing on his knee and singing "Bumpety bump, rider", which made Uncle Adi laugh. Miss Manziarly had set out sandwiches as well as cake and hot chocolate. Cheese and pickle. Uncle Adi didn't touch them. He ate three huge pieces of chocolate cake, one after the other, without stopping, or speaking, except to ask for more. When he'd finished, he drank his whole hot chocolate in one go. Then he pointed to a painting on the wall.

"Do you know who that is, Helga?"

I hate it when grown-ups do that. Even though we've done all those intelligence quizzes with Papa, I never seem to get used to being asked a question out of the blue in front of other people. I immediately feel stupid and sure that the answer that pops into my head must be wrong.

The painting is of a tired, nervous man with white curly hair and a big silver star on his jacket. Come to think of it, he looks rather like someone's just put him on the spot with a horrible question. I think I know who he is because Papa has a picture of him in his office; I just don't want to sound too certain in case I've got completely muddled.

"Frederick the Great?" I try to make my voice sound confident and curious at the same time, which doesn't really work.

"Clever girl!" (Phew). "Frederick the Great, and rightly so-called. He was the most outstanding man of his century. He understood how victory demands a great struggle. A great sacrifice. He lost all his teeth, you know. That was the strain of facing the Russian army. Our old enemies."

"Uncle Adi," said Helmut — he doesn't think a thing of interrupting — "how long till we beat the Russians?"

"Very soon!" Auntie Eva burst out before Uncle Adi had a chance.

"When are the new soldiers going to arrive?"

"Helmut, dear, don't bother Uncle Adi with all these questions. This is his time of day for resting." Mummy put her hand on his shoulder.

"Just one more question: when are you going to use the Wonder Weapons?"

Papa answered this time: "When the time is right, Helmut."

"Uncle Adi," Helmut continued, "which is your favourite Wonder Weapon? Mine is the Amerika rocket that will zoom through the stratosphere and smash down on New York. When is it going to be set off?" And he made a massive rocket-through-the-air-city-exploding noise to go with it.

Uncle Adi laughed, but he didn't answer Helmut's question. "You are a natural soldier, my boy, a natural soldier. What the people need to understand is that the Empire is like a patient with a critical illness. The patient has to take medicine. Sometimes the medicine is quite unpleasant; it takes time for the medicine to work; sometimes the patient feels like he is getting worse. But he must wait and trust that the medicine will work. The Empire will recover. It will be stronger than ever. Do you understand?"

"Yes, Uncle Leader."

"Clever boy, I wish my generals were as sensible as you."

Helmut beamed. I don't know if he did understand; I certainly didn't, but Uncle Adi's not the sort of person you like to question, because he says things with such certainty that you feel like you're an idiot if you don't understand.

After tea we still had an hour or so before bedtime and we were sitting in the corridor in the Upper Bunker, reading and trying to stay out of everyone's way, when we saw Mr. Speer.

I quite like Mr. Speer, but he always makes me feel shy. I think it's his eyebrows; they are so dark and thick and somehow unimaginable. Seeing him now though, I felt safe, and suddenly hopeful. Before we came into the bunker, I had overheard the servants saying that Mr. Speer had been trying to persuade Mummy and Papa to hide us from the Russians on a river barge. Maybe he'd come to get us. He greeted us with a small smile.

"What are you all up to?" he said, slipping his hands into his trouser pockets. I thought he might have sweets in them, but he didn't produce any.

I didn't know what to say, because he could see we were reading a story, but Heide answered and told him about our tea with Uncle Adi and our bath and the chocolate cake, babble, babble, babble…

It's only about ten days since we last saw Mr. Speer. He came to Swan Island to see Mummy. We were playing in the garden when he arrived, and he stayed and talked to us for a bit. We gave him a tour of all the daffodils and crocuses. He said that when he's an old man he will spend all his time gardening. Then he went inside to see Mummy, and he was with her for maybe an hour, anyway it seemed like ages, and then he left really quickly. His car was waiting and he just jumped into it with a very sharp wave to us, and was gone. I had the feeling he was angry. The next day his secretary, Miss Kempf, came. We hadn't met her before. She had tea with us and then she went alone with Mummy into the drawing room. When she came out I could see that she'd been crying. I asked Mummy later why Miss Kempf had been upset and she said that it was a private matter. It might all have been about escape plans, but I'm not sure.

Mr. Speer didn't look angry now. But he looked tired. Everybody looks tired. The bare light bulbs turn skin a yellowish grey.

"Is Grete here?" Hedda asked. Grete Speer is one of Hedda's best friends. They used to play together all the time before the Speers sold their house on Swan Island.

"No, I'm afraid not, I've come on my own."

"Where is she?" asked Hedda.

"Oh, in the mountains, they're all there with their mummy. So, do you have any paintings to show me?"

"Are they going to come here?"

"Ah, no. No. I don't think so. Little Ernst isn't very well, so they can't really go anywhere for a bit. Have you done any pictures of those lovely daffodils?"

I went to get our pile of drawings and paintings

from the bedroom, but by the time I got back Mr. Speer had gone. Apparently he'd been called through for a meeting with Uncle Leader. I didn't see him again, but in the evening I heard him outside our door with Papa.

"I had to come," I heard Mr. Speer say. "I had to see him one last time. He's looking tired. It's all over for him. But it's different for you. Your family. It's still possible to leave."

"We are staying with our Leader to the end," Papa replied.

"I'd like to talk to Magda."

"Indeed. I'll come with you."

"There's no need."

"No, really, I'll come."

I heard them knock on Mummy's door.

Afterwards Papa came to see us. He told us that Mr. Speer is leaving tonight.

"Can we go with him?" I asked.

"No, Helga. We're staying here till the war's over. It's the best place for us."

We're in Berlin. Nanny has put us to bed and Mummy has kissed us goodnight and turned out the light. Suddenly there's the sound of doors slamming. Mummy shouting, "Don't be ridiculous. They're asleep." Papa bursts into the room. "Helga, wake up! I've got something to show you." He picks me up. His coat is cold from the outside air. He carries me in my blanket downstairs, places me down on the sofa and goes to fetch the others. There's a man I don't know setting up a projector. Mummy is at the bottom of the stairs. "Josef, you're crazy. They'll be exhausted tomorrow! Helga's only just getting over her sore throat. You'll make her ill! And it won't be you dealing with all the tantrums tomorrow!"

Once we're all down, Papa squeezes into the middle of us and the man starts the film. It's the story of Snow White. It's in English but it's quite easy to understand if you know the basic story. It's not like any other film I've ever seen – it's a cartoon but it's very, very long and it's in colour. It's amazing. The Wicked Queen is so spooky and Snow White is so beautiful. It's a bit different from the fairy story because Snow White comes back to life when the Prince kisses her, and they missed out the ending where the Wicked Queen dances to death in red-hot shoes. It's an American film, but the original story is German. Papa says that at the moment the Americans are the best film-makers in the world but in ten years' time Germany will have overtaken them.

Later that year I had an operation which was supposed to stop me having so many sore throats. I remember getting ready to go to hospital. Mummy had bought me a little red suitcase, and a new nightdress, and a special bag for my toothbrush and flannel.

It was so exciting to be doing something just for me – none of the others were coming – and it was a really grown-up thing to do – Mummy and Papa often went to hospital, but none of us children had ever been to one except to be born, which obviously we couldn't remember. Me and Mummy got into the back of the car. Everything seemed particularly clear that day. The smell of the leather. The smell of her scent. She held my hand tightly and her rings dug into my fingers but I didn't say anything because I didn't want to let go of her lovely big safe hands.

As we went through the hospital doors we were immediately hit by the smell of disinfectant. Everything was black and white: the chequered floor tiles; the white sheets and black blinds; the nurses' black dresses and white aprons. We went up a big staircase to a small room with just one high metal bed and a little cupboard. Mummy helped me unpack my bag and then I had to take my clothes off and put on what they called a gown – like a stiff back-to-front cloak – which was a bit disappointing because I was looking forward to putting on my new nightie. Mummy was very smiley and chatty with the nurses, admiring everything – the good-quality linen, the height of the bed, the view from the window – "Oh look at the horse chestnuts!" – the sunshine – "Aren't we lucky!"

Mummy being so bright made me feel nervous. The doctor was a serious-looking man with little round glasses like Mr. Himmler. He didn't respond to Mummy's horse chestnut and lovely day comments. He looked at me intently, "You're just going to have a little injection to put you to sleep. You won't feel anything when we do the operation." Mummy squeezed one hand. The doctor took a firm grip of the other one. Suddenly I felt really scared – what if I was going to die? "Just a little scratch. There. Start counting to ten."

It was too late. One. Mummy's face dividing into squares. I didn't like this. Two. The doctor's glasses multiplying into bubbles. I never reached three. The next thing was a sudden sense of being awake and then opening my eyes and quickly closing them again against the bright light. A voice I didn't recognise was saying "Hello, Helga, hello, Helga," over and over again. Slowly I hauled myself up to the surface.

After the operation Granny B. looked after me at Swan Island. Granny B. is short for Granny Behrend.

That was the name she was born with, and she's gone back to it after getting divorced twice.

I lay with my feet up in a big deckchair and ate jelly and ice cream while Granny B. told me stories about when she was a chambermaid in a big hotel and how she had to get up in the dark and wash in cold water and then light the fires and heat the water for all the guests. "You don't know how lucky you are, young lady, sunning yourself in the lap of luxury."

I loved listening to Granny B.'s stories. Her kind voice kept up a soothing, steady rhythm which made everything seem alright. At some point that changed, but much later.

"When I was a child my family were very poor. My father died when I was about three years old, and my older sister must have been seven. My mother took in laundry and our rooms always smelt so wonderful, of soda flakes and hot irons. I remember when I was very young I would sit under the table, white sheets draped down the sides, as my mother pressed and ironed, and I would imagine I was in a snow castle.

"As soon as I was old enough, I think at about fourteen, I went to work as a maid for a large family who lived in a beautiful house on Bulow Strasse. My room was in the attic and I shared it with two other maids. One was a lady's maid, one was a kitchen maid and I was a chambermaid. In winter I was the first to rise, to clean out the fireplaces and light the day's fires. I was always afraid of oversleeping and I would lie in bed counting the chime of the church bells every hour.

"Your grandfather was a visitor to the house. He was a very elegant man, and very educated, a doctor of engineering. Immaculately dressed. I was particularly impressed that he wore a monocle in his left eye – all us girls considered a monocle to be a real mark of distinction.

"Of course, he travelled a great deal and when your mother was born he was living in Belgium. As you know he was a very generous man and for the first few years of your mother's life he supported us. I didn't have to work, I was able to look after your mother and we were very, very happy. She was a beautiful little girl with golden hair and big blue eyes. And very bright. I was so proud of her.

"It all came to an end when your mother was about five. I remember receiving the letter. Seeing the familiar handwriting, the thick cream envelope, the black ink, I expected it to contain, as usual, a generous cheque. But there was only a letter – thanking me for giving Magda such a good start in life. But now, the letter said, she was old enough to start her serious education and he had made arrangements for her to go to a convent school in Brussels. Would I please put her on such and such a train on such and such a day. From now on she would be his responsibility and I would be free to return to work.

"I felt sick. I remember just sinking down to the floor. I couldn't believe it. My beautiful girl was going to be taken away. And I had no choice. Without the money from your Grandpa Ritschel, there was no way I could afford to keep her. I read his words again and again: 'A good education will give our daughter the best chance in life. I know you would not wish to deprive her of this opportunity.'

"Anyway, the day came. I dressed her up warmly. Packed her food for the journey. I made a sign and hung it around her neck. Magda Behrend, Brussels. My name. He gave her money and education but not his name, not until later.

"I took her to the station. I told her she was going to see her father, and that I would see her soon. I couldn't bear to wave her off. I gave her to the guard, and he promised to find her a good seat, beside the window. She had been full of excitement that morning. Unable to eat her breakfast. But now she suddenly looked fragile, so tiny beside the burly guard. I didn't look back. I didn't want her to see me crying.

"I didn't see her again for two years. And it was much longer than that before I knew about her journey. I had given her a basket of food – apples and porridge and milk. I always insisted that she drink milk, because she was a skinny little girl and she needed building up. But she never liked her milk and apparently as soon as the train left the station she took the lid off the container and hurled the milk out of the window. It left a white streak which stayed there for the rest of the journey. If only I'd known that, I would have known she was alright, my brave little girl.

"Of course, I missed her terribly. And looking back I think I made a terrible mistake. I should have hidden my grief from Grandpa Ritschel, but I was desperate. I wrote to him almost every day, begging him to let me know where my little girl was. He wouldn't tell me the name of the convent. He thought I was going to steal her away. It was Grandpa Friedlander who made it possible for me to find my little girl again."

But I never met Grandpa Friedlander – he moved away before I was born. I don't know where.

It is only Grandpa Ritschel that I can remember. I was eight when he died. He used to send us little parcels of milk chocolate bars and pocket money. I remember him coming to tea in Berlin. It was a warm day and tea was served in the garden. He was very tall and he wore a straw hat, which he took off to eat. He told us about people in India who believe that we have many lives and that when we die we come back as someone or something else. He said he wanted to come back as an eagle. Mummy says he probably did.

Anyway, to keep herself busy, when she was missing Mummy so much, Granny B. got a job in a smart hotel. It was there that she met, and married, Grandpa Friedlander – he was the manager. He was a very kind boss, even though he was Jewish, and particularly kind to her. "Both my husbands were real gentleman," Granny B. always says.

Work at the hotel was very hard, the hours were very long, but at the end of the evening, when they finally went off duty, Granny B. and Grandpa Friedlander would go dancing.

"He was a beautiful dancer. For an hour or two I would forget my unhappiness. But it always came back and of course, Grandpa Friedlander realised. I remember the day I poured out my heart to him. We were walking around the lake at the zoo and I told him the story of your mother and how she had been taken from me. He didn't say anything at first. That was his way. He held my hand, and we walked and I cried. I don't think he had any words of comfort for me that day. But he took his time and quietly thought about it. A few days later, he had a plan. He would write to Grandpa Ritschel as my husband. He would give his assurance, man to man, that we would not take Magda away from him, nor would we deprive her of an education, but that if he would allow us to know where she was, we would move to Belgium, so that she could enjoy the love of both her parents.

"It was a brilliant plan. And he wrote a wonderful letter, full of confidence. He did not beg; he made a proposal. We posted the letter and we waited. I could hardly bear it. I was a bag of nerves, dying to hear the response. At last it came. Grandpa Ritschel agreed. If we moved to Belgium, he would let us know which school Magda was attending.

"I will never forget the day I saw my Magda again. The convent was a forbidding building. Huge. Grey stone. Pillars and columns. I immediately knew it was the wrong place for her. A nun opened the door and led us silently up a great wooden staircase to the Mother Superior's office. Your mother was waiting for us there and she was as thin as a stick. Instinctively, I rushed over to hug her but she shrunk back – and that broke my heart. She had been so starved of love in that cold, hard convent that she'd forgotten how to hug and be hugged. And then all she said, in a small voice was *Bonjour, Madame. Bonjour, Monsieur.*

"I had been dreaming of taking her in my arms and holding her, but I felt frozen.

"The Mother Superior invited us to sit down. She remained in the room. I immediately began to speak in German, telling Magda how I loved her, how much I missed her. Asking her how she was, how she found the convent. I probably burbled. The Mother Superior coughed. Magda remained silent.

"'All the girls speak French here.' The Mother Superior spoke hesitant German with a strong French accent. 'I think you will find that Magda has forgotten the language of her childhood.'

"She turned to Magda and said something to her in

French. Magda nodded, '*Oui, ma Mère.*'

"I don't know what I would have done without Grandpa Friedlander. He was such a gifted man. As well as Yiddish and German, he spoke fluent French. He turned to Magda, and explained to her something of what I had been trying to say. Of course, she didn't know him at all and it was a shock for her to discover I had a husband.

"We then set off on a tour of the school, guided by the Mother Superior. We were shown a series of well-polished classrooms. Magda held doors open and accompanied us politely, but she was as stiff as a stranger. The very last room we went to see was the dormitory. It turned out that all the girls slept in one large attic room. Rows and rows of beds. Magda's was in the middle. No curtain around it, no privacy, not even a wall to lean against and no protection from the cold draughts blowing in from the badly fitting windows. There was no ceiling, just the high eaves. It was absolutely freezing.

"Grandpa Friedlander arranged for us to return the following weekend. Magda shook our hands and said '*Au revoir.*' Her fingers felt cold and boney. We returned by train to our new, empty Brussels house. I cried and cried and cried.

"He was such a charming man, Grandpa Friedlander. He persuaded Grandpa Ritschel that Magda should move to a more comfortable convent. Grandpa Ritschel even allowed us to choose her next school, so long as it was Catholic. Although my mother had brought me up as a strict Protestant, and Grandpa Friedlander was, of course, Jewish, we happily agreed, and we started to visit convents.

"We finally found one where the dormitory was divided into cabins that could be closed off with curtains. Each girl had her own chair and her own wardrobe. We quickly arranged for Magda to move to this new school.

"It was, of course, very strictly Catholic. There was a great emphasis on modesty. When the girls had their weekly bath, the nuns insisted that they bathe in long gowns that completely covered their bodies. Even as they got in and out of the tub, the nuns deftly dried them and slipped on their chemises without revealing any flesh. No girl was supposed to see her own naked body.

"Every day started with mass before breakfast. Magda was still very skinny, with no reserves of strength. One morning at mass she fainted. After that I was allowed to bring her chocolate and she would eat one tiny piece before mass, to help her get through the service.

"The Mother Superior of the new school was a great woman. She loved music and she appreciated your mother's musical gift. Particularly her talent at the piano. She would take your mother to concerts and to museums and galleries. I think you could say your

74

mother was her favourite.

"Of course, that was a little difficult with the other girls. Magda never found it easy to make friends in Belgium. There was a lot of anti-German feeling, as we realised when war broke out.

"But for a few years we were happy. Grandpa Friedlander found good business opportunities. He opened a tobacconist's. We were comfortable. Gradually your mother began to recall her German. Her step-father helped with that, of course. And they became very close. He was more of a father to her than her real father. And it was her choice to take his name – Magda Friedlander.

"Then the war broke out – and everything changed. Your mother was now about twelve. We didn't under-stand the significance at first. We heard about the mur-der in Sarajevo. It seemed so far away, nothing that could affect us. But suddenly we realised that Europe was divided. Germany declared war on Russia, and then on France – Belgium's closest ally. Throughout Brussels, German shops were pelted with stones. All German civilians had to leave Belgium. We packed what we could carry. That was it.

"We were treated like animals. We went at first to the German consulate. There were so many of us – we were housed overnight in a circus tent. All kinds of people. We slept on the hard ground. Then the next morning we were marched to the station, by young Belgian soldiers – schoolboys really – who gave us coffee and chocolate and cigarettes from their own supplies. That was the last kindness we saw. We were sent back to Germany in cattle trains. Filthy, stinking cattle trains. It was absolutely foul. No seats, no windows. We sat on our suitcases. At times it was impossible to stretch out properly. There were no lavatories, no food and no water – though we were able to buy basic provisions at stations, it was very expensive and other people on the train had no money and would beg us to share what little we had. It took us six days to reach Berlin. Of course, people got ill and sick – it was disgusting. Human beings should never be treated like that. One woman, not in our carriage, but one down from us, even had a baby on the train. I can still remember her screaming and the rattling of the train through the night."

There is a story Mummy told me about this journey too. The train had stopped at a station when a Gypsy leapt aboard. She was as brown as a nut and as thin as a rake, with a great bundle of black hair escaping from a coin-fringed scarf. As soon as she entered the carriage, she fixed Mummy with her dark shining eyes. It was as if she could see right through to her soul, Mummy said. She grabbed Mummy's left hand and studied her palm. She traced her finger over its lines, then dropping the hand, looked Mummy in the eye.

"One day you will be a Queen of Life, but your ending will be dreadful!"

She turned and leapt off the train, just as it began to pull out of the station.

Mummy always laughs when she tells that story.

Day Four in the Bunker
Wednesday 25 April, 1945

Today started off badly. I woke up again in the night, thighs prickling with sweat. Instantly alert. Distant voices I couldn't make out. I shifted slowly so that my back was against the wall and at least I knew that nobody was going to come up behind me. I couldn't feel Elsa. I watched the slit of light under the door, looking for shadows and listening out for footsteps. Suddenly there were three loud explosions and everyone woke up. We switched on the light for a second to see the time – it was nearly five. Then the guns started. They are definitely getting louder. Are we just going to sit here waiting for the Russians to come and kill us?

All the time we were eating our breakfast there were soldiers carrying boxes out of the bunker. Boxes of what, and where they were taking them, I've no idea. I am bored of damson jam. So many stones. After breakfast I couldn't think of anything I wanted to do. Hilde is gripped by her Apache book, and she snuggled down with that – but I can't get in the mood to read. I asked Mrs. Junge if I could go and see Mummy. She said she'd ask. I just doodled and sat in the corridor, and the young ones played hide-and-seek again. I get this feeling of a weight pressing on my chest which makes me want to run and scream, but the worse thing is I know that won't make any difference. I covered a whole page in little black boxes and shaded them in. A waste of ink. I was about to embark on a second page when Mrs. Junge came and said that I could go and see Mummy.

Her room is like ours. Except the smell of diesel is mixed with the smell of cologne. It's completely bare. It reminds me of visiting her in the sanatorium.

She was lying in bed, her skin the same off-white as the pillows. Her eyes looked enormous for some reason, her pupils huge and black. She patted the side of her bed and I sat down, but it's so narrow that half of me was hanging off the bed. Her voice sounded flat.

"How are all you children?"

"We're fine. It's just so boring. How long are we going to be here?"

"I don't know, my darling. We will stay here as long as Uncle Leader needs to be here. Now, I've heard that you have all been very good and polite and no trouble. I'm very proud of you."

"How long is Uncle Leader going to stay here?"

"I don't know, darling."

"Are we going to try to escape?"

"Now you know we've brought you here because it's the safest place to be."

"What if the Russians get here?" I could feel a massive lump rising up in my throat and I just kept trying to swallow it, but I couldn't keep it down. I tightened my eyes as hard as I could to keep my tears in. My forehead felt like there was a sheet of metal pressing against it. I did manage not to cry, but I knew Mummy could tell that I almost was, and then I said it. "I'm so scared, Mummy. I don't want to die. I just really don't want to die."

Mummy hates it when we cry, which is unfair because she and Granny are always crying.

"Helga. Come on. Hold yourself together. You're a big girl. You must be strong for the little ones. You must give them a good example. Think how they will feel if they see that their big sister has been crying. This is not a time for tears. Remember you are German."

I concentrated and concentrated and breathed really slowly in and out of my mouth so that I didn't have to sniff. My jaw ached.

"Now, Helga, I am arranging for you all to have a vaccination. It's the same kind that all the soldiers have and I think that you children need it to stop you getting ill now that you are living cooped up like soldiers and so close to so many people."

I felt the shout inside me rising up but I swallowed it. I just said "Oh" in a small voice.

"I know you'll be brave, like a good girl, and not make a fuss."

I nodded. I couldn't really speak because of the giant lump in my throat. It sounded like she thought we were going to be here for a long time.

"I'm sorry you feel so bored. You'd better run along now and have your lunch. I'm going to get up later to have tea with Uncle Leader, and I will teach you a new game of patience. Now go and eat a good lunch, and don't let the others see you're upset."

Lunch was beef sandwiches. Holde carefully removed the meat and ate the bread and butter. Helmut ate her meat. I just couldn't think of anything drearier in the whole world than beef sandwiches. The brownness of it all seemed unbearable. I never thought I'd miss vegetables – but it would be so nice to have something bright and fresh like peas or even carrots, something light and happy and not just chewy heavy dead cow and chewy heavy dead bread. Of course, I didn't say anything. I ate it very slowly until I had a huge dry lump of meat in my cheek. When Mrs. Junge turned away to speak to a soldier I spat it into my napkin. I never want to eat beef again in my whole life. I'm going to be vegetarian like Uncle Leader.

After lunch we went for our rest. I got straight into my bunk and pulled the covers over my head and then

I couldn't breathe. I made a little air gap, but kept my face hidden. I don't know why I feel so tired when we're not doing anything.

Liesl came to get us ready for tea. She redid my plaits and tied the bow at the back of my dress and gave me a little hug. I feel like a four-year-old in this outfit. Short sleeves that give my arms goose pimples, short white socks. All us girls matching. I can't wait till I'm a grown-up and I can choose my own clothes. I'm going to have long, loose, swishy hair and high heels and a navy-blue, polka-dot skirt. After the war Mummy says I can be fitted for a bra. I almost need one now.

The others are still pretty chirpy. Helmut remains convinced that this is all great fun. Holde and Hedda and Heide were a bit quiet for the first day or so but now they are all excited about cake and puppies and they love Mrs. Junge and the teddies and they are pretty well fine. Sometimes they get really scared of the explosions, but then they seem to forget all about them. I wish I could talk to Hilde, but it's almost like she's not here. She hardly ever wants to play cards or board games, or do anything together. All she wants to do is read. She carries her on-the-go book everywhere, and as soon as she's finished one she's on to the next. And she does this really annoying thing with her cheeks. She sucks them in three times before she does anything – before she gets out of bed, takes off her nightie, puts on her pants, everything. She looks like a fish.

If this is such a safe place I'm sure Mr. Speer would have brought his children here instead of sending them into the mountains. And what about Edda Goering? She'd definitely be here. She has to have the best of everything. And Mr. Bormann hasn't got his children here with him. Why is it just us?

Tea came and went again. Auntie Eva had her painted smile and her glittering diamonds. Uncle Adi had made less of an effort with his appearance. As soon as we got there, he asked Mrs. Junge to fetch the puppies. At first I thought he was talking to me because he said, in quite a gentle voice, "Child, bring in the dogs." But she leapt up.

We all played with the puppies on the floor. Foxl snuggled his nose into my armpit. Uncle Adi didn't ask any difficult questions about school or German history. He just talked about the dogs. He said he prefers dogs to people because you can always trust them, they never lie, they are always loyal and always obedient. He made Blondi do her schoolgirl trick again, but when he went to pat her on the head, he spilt his hot chocolate all over his lap. He immediately went purple red and started shouting furiously. Auntie Eva leapt over and started dabbing him with her inadequate little lace handkerchief, which made him even more furious. Mummy whispered fiercely, "Back to your room, children!" Mrs. Junge came with us. She told us he often calls his secretaries "child", especially her because she's the youngest. I think she's 25 – not young at all.

We fiddled about in the corridor for a bit and then Mummy came up and showed me the new patience. It's quite good. You have a pile of thirteen cards you can't look at and then you deal out four and – well, it's difficult to explain, but basically you have to make suits. I played it quite a few times. I like the flicky sound of the cards as you turn them over in threes. It never worked out, but there's a nice feeling of fresh hope every time you start a new deal.

1940

We went to Castle Lanke, Papa's official country house, for New Year. Swan Island is our private one. I prefer the private one.

The weather was absolutely freezing. Thick, crusty snow which squeaked when you walked on it. Papa and Mummy gave us new toboggans for Christmas – really good ones, big enough for grown-ups to go on. Papa came with us. He was the fastest, but he got really angry when he fell off. We had to make sure we didn't laugh.

Mummy doesn't like tobogganing, but she came with us for a sleigh ride in the forest. We covered ourselves in fur rugs. When it snows the forest around Castle Lanke becomes a fairyland. The tall dark trees, draped in their snow shawls, stoop like old witches. After a bit the whiteness begins to hurt your eyes. Back home we had hot chocolate by the fire and Papa told us stories about when he was little.

"My earliest memories are of nightmares, of lying feverish in bed, one minute thinking that the walls were moving in to crush me, the next minute feeling myself stuck in sinking mud, unable to free my feet. I remember the room. Heavy green curtains that turned to trees in my dreams. Strangling ferns and fronds on the wallpaper. I must have been about four. I had a bone disease. My right foot developed a terrible cramp, a searing pain. I can remember lying in bed and concentrating my very hardest to move my toes. It was impossible. Whenever I smell almond oil I feel myself back on that bed, staring at the ceiling, as my mother rubbed and pummelled my leg.

"And then there were the doctors' appointments. So much sitting and waiting on hard seats below high windows you could never see out of. All I wanted to do was run about like other children. I remember we even made the journey to Bonn, to the University Medical School. My mother told me that we were going to see the cleverest doctors in the world. I had to lie on a bed with my trousers off surrounded by a dozen young men who took turns at lifting and pinching my foot to see what I could feel. But could they help me? Not a bit. They came up with this clumpy contraption that was meant to hold my foot straight and help me to walk. Ha. That went down well at school. The Little Cripple looked just the part with his orthopaedic appliance.

"My mother, of course, like any good Catholic woman, looked to God as well as to doctors in her search for a cure. Every day after school, while the other boys ran off to play football, the Little Cripple was met at the school gates by his mother, who took his hand and walked him down to St. Mary's church. We would kneel together in this cold dark cavern for up to an hour. I knelt in silence, hiding my face in my hands, as my mother, over and over again, beseeched 'Our Lady, to pray for us to the Lord our God'.

"'What have I done to deserve this punishment, oh Lord? Please forgive me my sins and the sins of my son. Have mercy, Lord, and remove this evil from us. Dear Jesus, healer of the sick, restore your servant to health. We beg for forgiveness. Have mercy, Lord.'

"I remember one particular day. It was summer, a beautiful day, the kind of day I most resented spending in the gloomy church. As we went out into the street we met a large lady called Mrs. Backer who ran the Sunday school.

"'Good afternoon, Mrs. Goebbels. Praying to the good Lord in your affliction again? If anyone deserves forgiveness it is you, Mrs. Goebbels. No one could question your devotion. Still the Lord moves in mysterious ways. Who are we to understand the trials and punishments he sends us?'

"'Indeed, Mrs. Backer,' my mother replied. 'Prayer is a great comfort to me. But you know Josef's foot was hurt in a simple accident. It was not sent as an affliction. He caught his foot in the slats of a bench when I was lifting him. A silly accident, but not a punishment, Mrs. Backer – a human error, not a divine intervention.'

"'Indeed, Mrs. Goebbels. I didn't mean to imply…'

"As we hurried home I asked my mother to tell me the story of the slatted bench. I had never heard this before. My mother shushed me until we were inside and then she explained.

"'There are ignorant people in this town,' she said. 'People who believe that God sends illness to punish evil. If I tell them it is my fault that you're a cripple, they can call us stupid, they can call us careless, but they can't call us evil.'

"When I was ten my mother found a doctor who thought that he could cure my foot by an operation to reshape it. The bone would be broken and reset straight. I would be able to walk normally.

"After the operation I had three weeks' rest in the hospital. I was not allowed to leave my bed. I thought I would die of boredom, but my godmother and aunt Christina came to visit me on the second day and she brought me a present which quite honestly changed my life. It was a book of fairy tales. I had never read a fairy tale before – now I devoured them – Hansel and Gretl, Snow White and Rose Red, Rapunzel... I read them and reread them. These stories awakened my love of reading. I asked the nurses to bring me anything they could find for me to read – even old newspapers, I didn't care if I could understand or not. I just wanted to read. My father immediately realised that my love of reading could be a great advantage, and he brought me an encyclopaedia. I read it from cover to cover and, when at last I returned to school, I reaped the rewards. Suddenly I was a clever boy. I knew more than anyone else in the class. I was no longer just a sad cripple. I was someone to respect, someone who could help the other boys with their homework, someone the teachers liked. At last, I had a future. The operation, of course, had been a failure."

In Berlin we used to have a maid called Gerda. She was one of those people who always look a bit grubby no matter how hard they try. It used to drive Mummy mad. Strands of hair would always escape her bun. Her stockings would always ladder. Her fingernails were always dirty. Mummy said she was a slut and had to be kept out of sight of guests; she just did fires and cleaning, but Mummy kept Gerda because she was strong and could get a better shine on the brass than any of the other maids. We all liked Gerda because if no one else was around she would let us do things that were normally forbidden – like bouncing on beds – or she'd sneak us up biscuits from the kitchen, even if it was just before lunch and we were supposed to be saving our appetites. I always felt a bit awkward, half glad to have the treat, yet feeling guilty that we were disobeying Mummy behind her back, but the little ones simply adored her, especially Hilde.

One day we were playing in the dining room and we heard terrible screaming coming from the kitchen. Nanny came in and shooed us up to our bedroom. She wouldn't tell us a thing. She wasn't one of my favourite nannies that one. Very thin and screechy. The next day there was no sign of Gerda and we never saw her again.

No one would tell me what had happened. I heard Nanny saying that she'd brought it on herself, falling for a Jew boy – and personally she thought it was a good thing that Mr. Goebbels was clearing Berlin of these undesirable elements. We got a new maid, Elvira, and her hair was so tidy that you could see the comb marks in it. I heard her telling Nanny that there was no way she was going to lose her head over a boy and stick it in an oven. I had this image of Gerda cutting off her head and cooking it. I begged Cook to explain what had happened, but she would only tell me that Gerda was fine, I wasn't to worry, but she was a silly girl and Mummy was quite right to send her packing. "We can't be having any more dramatics." All Mummy would say was that Gerda was a weak and selfish girl and we were better off without her. Weak was the one thing I thought Gerda wasn't.

I remember Heide being born. It was late at night and we were all in bed. It was Papa's birthday and he was having a party downstairs. Loud gramophone music and loud laughter, Papa's laughter being the loudest of all. Earlier in the evening we'd looked down over the banister and watched the guests arrive – beautiful actresses in beautiful dresses. Mummy wasn't there. She'd been in hospital for weeks, partly because of being pregnant and partly because of her bad heart. Suddenly Papa came bursting into the nursery.

"Wake up! Wake up! Mummy's had a baby. We're going to see her. Nanny, coats on top of nighties."

"Is it a boy?" Helmut had been longing for a brother.

"No, Helmut, it's a little girl. I'm afraid you and me and Harald are completely outnumbered. Let's go."

I remember there was a car waiting for us, but it hadn't warmed up. We only had our night things under our coats so we shivered all the way to the hospital. Mummy was propped up in bed. She started crying when we went in. Papa told her to "Buck up, sweetie" and left us to comfort her while he went in search of a nurse to fetch the baby. He came back with the baby in his arms and started dancing around the room. "Josef, please, you'll disturb her. You're not at a party now."

Papa carried on dancing. The baby didn't wake up. In the end he gave her to Mummy to hold and we were able to get a proper look. Her face was all squashed up and chinless. Mummy told us that she was going to be called Heide and Helmut raced around the room shrieking "Heide, Heide, Hi diddly dee!"

Mummy started crying again. Papa said it was time to go home.

Day Five in the Bunker
Thursday 26 April, 1945

After a whole day without anyone new coming into the bunker – which made me think that we were completely cut off from the rest of Germany and from safety in our strange bunker world – today brought a dramatic arrival.

We were playing with the puppies in Auntie Eva's room – I don't know where Auntie Eva was, but Liesl was there doing the ironing – when we heard a commotion in the corridor, shouting and doors banging, and before Liesl could stop us, we ran out to have a look at what was going on. There were six soldiers carrying a stretcher. Beside them was a little woman with a very loud voice yelling orders: "Move on! Get out of the way! Where's the doctor?" She was wearing a massive leather jacket that didn't fit her at all, a man's jacket, I think, on top of a very torn flying suit. The soldiers carried the stretcher into the doctor's room at the end of the corridor. We saw Dr. Stumpfegger hurrying down from the Upper Bunker. He has a very strange run; it all happens below the knees while his upper body remains completely still. He gives me the creeps. He is very tall and skinny and pale, as if he is barely alive, and his eyes are always cast down at the floor. Mummy says he's one of the cleverest doctors in the world.

On the stretcher was a large man shielding his eyes with one hand. We could only really see the top of his balding head and his thin grey hair. His body was covered by a blood-stained army blanket. Liesl quickly scooped us back into Auntie Eva's room. She didn't know who these visitors were. My first thought was that if these people had been able to get in then it must still be possible for us to get out. And then I thought it looked like it had nearly killed them to get here.

Eventually Auntie Eva came back to her room. Mummy was with her. It turns out that the bossy little woman is Hanna Reitsch. Which makes sense. You probably need to be the world's greatest pilot to get past the Russian anti-aircraft guns. Mummy says she's incredibly brave. I've seen her in news films, she can do amazing stunts, but I didn't recognise her. If anyone could fly us out of here, I reckon she could. Unfortunately, Auntie Eva says that Flight Captain Reitsch (apparently she insists on being called Flight Captain and won't answer to Miss) plans to stay beside the Leader until the end of the war. She also told us that the injured man is another top pilot – General Robert Ritter von Greim. Maybe he could get us out, if he recovers in time. Auntie Eva and Mummy say that Dr. Stumpfegger will be able to stitch up the General.

Flight Captain Reitsch was sitting on the sofa next to Uncle Leader when we went down to tea. Foxl was on her lap, but I'm glad to say he jumped down and came waggling towards me as soon as we came in. The Flight Captain had washed and changed and was wearing a dress of Auntie Eva's that was ridiculously big and dragging over her feet. She is really tiny except for her teeth, which we saw a lot of as she guffawed at Blondi's tricks.

She told us the story of her journey here. The General had received the Leader's summons to the bunker and had ordered Reitsch to come with him. They set off from Munich in a tiny plane called a Focke-Wulf. The same pilot who had brought Mr. Speer here agreed to fly them to Berlin. There was only just room for the pilot and one passenger, so the General squeezed in next to the pilot and Flight Captain Reitsch had to lie down on the floor in the tail of the plane. They flew very low and they had 40 Luftwaffe fighter planes flying beside them to protect them. By the time they arrived at Gatow airport on the edge of Berlin, nearly all the fighter planes had been shot down. At Gatow they got into an even smaller plane, one which would be small enough to land in the middle of Berlin. The General took the controls and Flight Captain Reitsch sat beside him. The pilot refused to come any further. They flew so low that they could see the faces of the soldiers fighting in the streets below. Suddenly some Russians turned their guns on the plane. The bullets ripped right through the side of the plane and hit the General's foot. Flight Captain Reitsch had to lean over him and grab the controls. Amazingly, she managed to land the plane from the passenger seat.

Helmut was very excited. He now says he wants to be a pilot, like Harald. Hanna Reitsch promised him that she would teach him to fly after the war.

Apparently Uncle Leader had told her that we were wonderful singers so she got us to sing "Night Silence" and "Can You Count the Stars?". Auntie Eva had a headache and went for a rest after "Night Silence", which was lucky because Heide then volunteered a solo performance of "Ladybird, Ladybird", which was a high- pitched racket.

Hanna Reitsch guffawed some more and asked if she would be allowed to put us to bed because she would love to teach us some more songs. Mummy said, "Yes – but no more exciting stories – the children need to be calm at bedtime."

Auntie Eva recovered from her headache and came with Hanna Reitsch to put us to bed. I wished it had been Mummy, but she was resting.

First of all Flight Captain Reitsch taught us the dwarves' yodelling song from *Snow White,* which was all ho-de-lays and yodels. Helmut got hysterical giggles so she tried to calm us down with a rather childish lullaby.

Sleep, baby, sleep!
Your father guards the sheep,
Your mother shakes the little tree,
Down falls a little dream for thee,
Sleep, baby, sleep!

Sleep, baby, sleep!
Two sheep are there outside,
A black one and a white one,
And when the child doesn't want to sleep,
The black one comes and bites him!
Sleep, little child, sleep

We sang it through once together and then she divided us into two groups and we sang it as a two-part harmony. We had to stick our fingers in our ears so that we didn't get confused by what the others were singing. She says that we should sing it to Uncle Leader tomorrow.

After the singing she tucked us all in. I asked her, really quietly so that I wouldn't put ideas in the others' heads, whether she thought it would be possible to fly us out of here. She said she thought that this was the best place to be. She wants to stay here herself and support Uncle Leader, but even if she did have to fly out on his orders, it would be in a tiny plane and it would be impossible for her to take us with her.

Everyone keeps saying that this is the best place to be, an honour to be with the Leader and so on, and nobody seems to be thinking about what we will do if our troops don't manage to force back the Russians.

Flight Captain Reitsch turned out the light and left us. I can't get the yodelling tune out of my head.

Papa showed us a new film he'd made, called *The Eternal Jew*. It's all about Jews and what they believe and how they live. It's revolting. It shows you all the bugs and dirt in Jewish houses, and how Jews are like rats, but they can disguise themselves to look like normal people, so you have to be very careful. Papa told us that they were planning to introduce a law which would make Jews wear a yellow badge on their coats so that they could be easily recognised. The idea comes from England, where it was used hundreds of years ago. It stops Jews pretending that they're normal and deceiving people, and makes it easier to round up the Jews and send them all out of the country, which is what they did in England in the end, though they let them back later.

The film dragged on a bit and all the others fell asleep. Suddenly there was a warning on the screen: *Don't watch the next bit if you are sensitive!* Papa said he thought I was old enough to watch it.

It was about Jewish butchery. It showed these Jews killing a cow. It was unbelievably disgusting. They took this long, sharp knife and with one sudden slash they slit the cow's throat. Blood poured out. I couldn't believe that cows had so much blood; hot, steaming blood. The poor cow made a feeble attempt to raise itself and then just lay twitching for ages till it died.

Papa says that Uncle Leader is going to make this kind of killing illegal. I asked Papa if I could become a vegetarian like Uncle Leader but he said not until I'm 21. He promised that we would never eat meat that's been killed by Jews.

I asked Papa whether Grandpa Friedlander was like the Jews in the film. He got very angry and told me that I was never to call him that, he wasn't my grandpa, and he wasn't a person we talked about. He said Granny B. was exactly the sort of person who needed the yellow-badge law to protect her and to stop her from mixing with the wrong people. I didn't mention the Jewish friends I knew Mummy had when she was growing up.

After the war broke out in 1914, Mummy and Granny B. and Grandpa Friedlander – I don't know what else I could call him, I don't even know his first name – returned to Berlin and went to live in a large villa. Each room had been assigned to refugees. Single people had to share, but because they were a family the Friedlanders had a room to themselves – one of the upstairs bedrooms. There was nowhere to cook, so every lunchtime Mummy went with her mother to a Red Cross soup kitchen and joined the queue for hot food. Grandpa Friedlander spent every day looking for work, eventually finding a position in a top hotel. They were now able to afford a little flat. They found one in a Jewish quarter where Grandpa Friedlander had lived before they went to Brussels. Mummy started at the nearby school.

Although Mummy now spoke fairly good German, she still thought in French. She could understand the teachers but when she answered questions her sentences would start in German and finish in French. No one thought this particularly strange, because a lot of the students were refugees, speaking German as a second language. Granny B. says this was the first time Mummy really made friends.

"There was a girl called Lisa, a neighbour of ours. She would walk home from school with your mother and most days they ended up going back to Lisa's flat to do their homework together. Lisa's family had originally escaped from Russia. Her father had died there, but Lisa's mother was a strong woman and she managed to make a good life for herself and her son and two daughters in Berlin. Your mother loved to visit them. Their apartment was always full of young people. Lisa's older brother, Victor, was quite a character – very political, even at that age. Passionate about Palestine. He believed that there should be a Jewish homeland in Palestine – they called it Zion. At the time I thought it was a pipe dream – youthful enthusiasm – but looking back I think he was right. As we have all come to realise, Germany is not the best place for

Jews. They don't fit in here.

"Anyway, it was more fun for your mother at the Arlosoroffs' than it was at home, being an only child. Like your mother, they were very musical, always singing songs around the piano. And Victor used to hold all these weekly meetings for Zionists. Your mother used to go. She got quite swept up by it all. You have to remember this was the war. Food was short. You had to queue for hours for bread, and when you got it, it tasted like the rye had been mixed with sawdust. It was hard to see the light at the end of the tunnel. The news from the front wasn't good. These young Jewish people, well, their group was actually called "Hope of Zion" – they had hope, they had a dream of a better world, and your mother loved that. And then, of course, there was Victor himself: not a good-looking boy, well, I never thought so – uncontrollable hair and round black glasses – but there was no denying his energy, his authority. Rather like your father in that way. He was a natural leader. I think they all saw him as the first leader of the new homeland they were going to create.

"Your mother fell for him, utterly. I first had an inkling of her feelings on her fifteenth birthday. Grandpa Friedlander brought her a cake from the hotel. Oh, it was wonderful – real white flour, flavoured with a little cocoa – which was very scarce because of the English blockades. It was as light as a feather. So, we had a little birthday tea – the three of us and Lisa and Dora Arlosoroff. It was lovely.

"The next day Magda came straight back from school. Without even taking off her coat she opened the cake tin. 'Mama, there's still lots of cake left. You and me and Papa will never finish it. I'm going to take it round to the Arlosoroffs'.'

"'Well,' I said, 'that's very sweet of you, but don't you think Lisa and Dora had enough yesterday?'

"'Maybe, but Victor didn't get any. He loves cake.'

"With that she was back off out the door, cake tin under her arm, satchel lying by the front door where she had dropped it. She wasn't the kind of girl to ask permission before she did something. If she knew what she wanted to do, she did it.

"It must have been a year or two later that your mother came bursting into our bedroom after an evening at the Arlosoroffs'. 'Mama, Papa – I have the most marvellous news! Victor has asked me to marry him. And I have accepted. Not now, of course. We are going to save up to move to Palestine. We will make a new life there, not just for ourselves, but a new society – one without poverty or oppression!'

"I don't know, young people always think they have all the answers. And what she thought she was going to save up, I have no idea. She was still a schoolgirl. But there, she had her dreams and they made her happy.

"The war ended on the day your mother was

seventeen. But it was not the victory we had been expecting. There was a strange atmosphere in Berlin. Marches and street fights. You could hear gunshots. Bands of marauding sailors. It was dangerous. I remember your mother being sent home early from school because the streets weren't safe. Of course the King abdicated. It felt like the country was falling apart. We couldn't believe we'd lost – and on what terms – it was a humiliation. And the thing was, we all knew we hadn't lost the fight. We weren't invaded. Our defences weren't broken. No. It was not the war we had lost. It was the peace negotiations. Everyone said we'd been stabbed in the back. The enemy didn't defeat us, we were betrayed. Naturally a lot of people blamed the Jews. People said that they had been busy making money instead of fighting for the fatherland. It wasn't true in our neighbourhood. We knew several Jewish boys who had lost their lives fighting – poor Hans Silberstein was the first. A nice boy. And as for the supposed wealth of the Jews – well, there was little sign of it around us. But there were incidents, tensions. Smashed windows. Spitting in the street. It wasn't an easy time being married to a Jew, I must say, and that took its toll. It was bound to.

"Your mother had by now left school and she persuaded Grandpa Ritschel to send her to a finishing school. She thought it would open the door to grand society. She got ever so cross with me because she felt I should have had a place arranged for her as soon as she left school.

"'You can't stand in the way of my destiny. What do you expect me to do? Take in needlework and spend the rest of my life in the Berlin suburbs? Well I'm going to make something of myself and you can't hold me back!' All sorts of histrionics we had.

"Of course, the truth was that I didn't have the funds for one of these finishing schools, but in the end she persuaded Grandpa Ritschel. He kitted her out with a new wardrobe, the latest fashion, everything she could possibly need to become a smart young lady. Off she went to this academy in the mountains – to be finished. Naturally, it was rather a disappointment. Very strict and snooty. It can't have helped having a surname like Friedlander. I remember her excitement when she returned for her first holiday. It was only for a few days. She had been given special permission to come home for Grandpa Friedlander's birthday. Victor was 21 a few days later, and she was able to stay for his party too. She was glowing. All her beautiful clothes. Her new bobbed haircut. She was thrilled to be back in Berlin and to see all her friends. We had a lovely dinner for Grandpa Friedlander and we sang all the old folksongs. And then of course there was Victor's party.

"I've never got to the bottom of what happened that night. She went off happily enough in a lovely silver dress and a big silk rose in her hair. She looked beautiful. But, most unlike her, she came back early. I heard her slamming the front door as I was getting ready for bed. I knew it wasn't worth going to see what the matter was. She would never talk when she was upset. I thought it would have just blown over by the morning. But no, she was still in a terrible mood at breakfast. She pushed her porridge around the bowl. Glared at the table. Barely said goodbye to Grandpa Friedlander.

"I took her to the station, silence all the way, and then – even though we were there in fairly good time – we couldn't find her a seat. Every one that was empty had a reserved ticket on it. I left her with her bags beside a reserved compartment up at one end of the train and walked right to the other end to see if I could find a single seat. By the time I got back she was sitting comfortably inside the compartment chatting away to two gentlemen.

"'Mother, I have been rescued. These two gentleman have very kindly invited me to join them. Let me introduce you – my mother, Mrs. Friedlander – Dr. Quandt and Mr. Schwartz.'

"'Please, there's no need to thank us. We were expecting to be joined by some colleagues who have now decided to travel tomorrow. It is a pleasure to meet you.'

"The man she had introduced as Dr. Quandt leapt up to shake my hand. He was a man about my age, quite stout and obviously quite bald despite some careful combing, but with brilliant blue eyes. I had no idea then that he was one of the most successful businessmen in Germany, but I could tell immediately that he was an exceptional man. What struck me most was how extraordinarily like Grandpa Ritschel he looked.

"There was no sign now of Magda's black mood. She kissed me warmly and off I went, with no other thought in my head other than how nice it was that she had recovered her temper before she left.

"The next time I saw her must have been about three weeks later. She turned up in Berlin unannounced. Now, Grandpa Friedlander had been ill. My sister, who lived in Magdeburg, had had her first grandchild and my niece Konstanze had sweetly asked me to be godmother. Unfortunately, I couldn't leave my husband. He was very frail. So I asked Magda to represent me as godmother and again she got special permission to leave school for the family event. She was supposed to return to her school straight from the christening. However, she did no such thing, but made her way to Berlin.

"So she arrived home out of the blue, early one morning, having travelled overnight. She announced that she had no intention of going back to finishing school. I was naturally concerned.

"'It doesn't matter what you say, there is no question of me going back to that place.'

"'But Magda, your father has spent a great deal of money to send you there. You can't just throw away this opportunity. You don't know how lucky you are to be living in the beautiful Harz mountains. Most Berlin girls would give their eye teeth to have such an experience.'

"'The beautiful Harz mountains! Oh yes, we've had some lovely walks in the mountains. In the mist. The only thing I've seen of the Harz mountains is the shoes of the girl climbing in front of me. I've greater things in my sights. As you will see.'

"The following weekend your mother and I were invited to visit Gunther Quandt at his lakeside villa. Grandpa Friedlander was now well enough to be left, but not well enough to join us so there was no embarrassment in the fact that he was not invited.

"The villa was out of this world. An elegant mansion with windows reaching from floor to ceiling looking out over immaculate parkland stretching down to the lake. 'My dear,' I whispered to Magda, 'I understand the attraction.'

"It was the wrong thing to say. She took me aside, glaring furiously, 'Make no mistake, Mother, I won't marry him if I don't love him.'

"But she did. They announced their engagement that summer, on his 39th birthday. He was now a little more than twice her age. He was a widow. His wife had died in the influenza epidemic after the war. He had two sons, Helmut and Herbert, eleven and thirteen at the time, I think.

"They married in January 1921. Your half-brother Harald was born later that year. Your mother converted to Protestantism to marry Gunther and she changed her surname before the wedding. She married as Magda Ritschel. Gunther didn't want to marry a woman with a Jewish name. Things had become difficult between myself and Grandpa Friedlander and in fact, we parted at much the same time. It was becoming impossible to carry on. The world had changed. The position of Jews had changed. Gunther didn't want a Jew at the wedding. He didn't want to be associated with them. I had to decide between my daughter's world and my husband's world – obviously my daughter had to come first."

❧❧❧

I think it was when I was about eight that Uncle Leader's war really started affecting our lives. Before that there'd been a bit of bombing, which I thought was quite exciting, but from this point the war became annoying. We had to go and stay with the Goerings in Upper Salt Mountain. Mummy thought that we weren't getting enough sleep because of the air raids in Berlin.

The Goerings are ghastly. Luckily Empire Marshall Goering – Uncle Herman, as we were told to call him – was hardly ever there. He is disgustingly fat; he always has little globs of sweat on his pudgy face and he breathes really loudly as if he's about to die. Auntie Emmy, the High Lady, as all the servants call her, is all silk and talcum powder and wafts in and out of rooms in flowing lavender dresses. When she talks she pats her hair and gazes into the distance and her words float away before you can catch them. Most of the time she was away too, visiting her older children in Switzerland. Eddakins, their golden girl, was about three years old then. Silly little curls and vile spoilt behaviour.

Their house in Upper Salt Mountain appears to be on top of the world. Even though you look out over huge snowy mountains you feel like you are in the sky. The house itself is like an enormous cottage, something out of a fairy tale on the outside, but inside everything is modern and plush – lots of rugs and unnecessary little tables and glass ashtrays which you aren't allowed to touch. There are lawns and woods, a swimming pool. Supposedly everything you might want. I don't know why it's horrible but it is.

We'd only been there two days when Mummy told us at breakfast that she would have to leave after lunch to go to her clinic in Dresden to rest her heart. I just remember feeling completely sick. None of the others seemed to be listening. She said, "Miss Oda will look after you until I am well enough to come back. It won't be long." But it was obvious it would be.

We all hated Miss Oda. We nicknamed her Ear

Phones because she had a spiral of plaited hair wound over each ear, and she was such a phoney. She was always really polite in front of Mummy or the Goerings, and then really rude when they weren't there. She called Auntie Emmy a Jew lover. "The High Lady's abandoned us, hasn't she, Eddakins? Swanned off to her Jew friends and left us with these young hooligans. Nobody asked me if I could look after them. No. Mummy and Papa can't cope with the little darlings so they dump them on us. I'm worn out with running round after refugees. Do I get any thanks? No. And as for Little Miss (that was me) – she thinks she's the cat's whiskers. She's a sly little devil, blubbing on the phone to Mummykins, making out she's all hard done by. Spoilt to death, if you ask me."

Edda Goering was just as horrid and always trying to get us into trouble: "Odie, Odie, Helmut's being mean to me." Odie Ear Phones always believed her and Helmut would be sent to stand in the corner. It was so unfair. He would try really hard not to cry because if there was the slightest hint of tears, Ear Phones would start singing:

Cry, baby, cry
Stick your finger in your eye
Tell your mother it wasn't I!

Mummy phoned once a week. Sometimes Papa phoned.

"Mummy," I'd whisper, "Miss Oda is really mean."

"Come on, Helga. Don't tell tales. Have you had fun tobogganing?"

"I hate it here. Why can't we come back to Berlin? I don't mind the air raids."

"Helga. There is a war on. We all have to make sacrifices. Now don't make a fuss, I don't want you upsetting the others. Can I speak to Holde now?

Every day we had the same routine. Morning lessons with Mrs. Kleinwort, who was 200 years old and walked with a stick that she tapped on the floor angrily if someone, usually Helmut, wasn't paying attention. She had a quavery voice and she was always saying, "Come, come, come, we studied this yesterday." Mornings lasted for ever.

Lunch was the highlight of the day. There were always puddings – apple strudel, rice pudding, jam tarts, all served with lots of thick yellow cream. At home our food was rationed, like everyone else's in Germany. Mummy explained that the English were trying to starve us by stopping food ships from reaching Germany, so all the food in the country had to be shared fairly, to make sure everyone had something. Papa had even announced on the radio that anyone who ate more than their ration would be executed. It's very serious. If we don't share fairly Germans will die. Butter, milk, eggs, meat and jam are all rationed and each person only gets a tiny bit. At home Cook has sorted out the fridge so that we all have our own section for keeping our rations to make sure that we don't eat up each other's. Actually, it isn't fair because Heide and Hedda and Holde get more milk and eggs because they're younger, which I think is ridiculous because I've got a much bigger tummy to fill.

Anyway, no one seems to have told the Goerings that they will be killed if they don't stick to rations. They have an endless supply of butter and cream and milk from their farm – and lots of other things we hadn't been able to have for ages, like bananas and oranges and sweets and chocolates. I don't know where they get them from. I decided to make the most of it, while we were there, and not feel too guilty, because I couldn't really take my dollop of cream down the mountain to the villagers – and also food was the only thing to look forward to at the Goerings'.

After lunch every day we would have a rest – I never needed to sleep but there was absolutely nothing to read – there are no good books in the Goering house and we soon got through the ones we took with us. Then we would have an hour of compulsory outdoor play, whatever the weather. Edda was usually able to wriggle out of it – or rather whine out of it – but we never were. This was followed by a huge tea of chocolate or apple cake, sometimes jam doughnuts, even ginger biscuits. Then instrument practice, indoor play, bread and butter and cocoa and finally bath and bed.

Exactly the same every day. No outings. No surprises. So an awful lot of time to think about how much I was missing Mummy and Papa.

We all shared one big nursery room with six beds in it, and little Edda had her own bedroom and bathroom, all painted pink. By her bed was a massive photograph of the hundreds of airplanes that flew over Berlin to celebrate her birth. Her father arranged this big display because he was head of the air force.

Mummy was gone ages. When she left us there it was winter, when she came back it was summer. When she finally came, she came to take us away. I don't know what made her realise at last that we couldn't bear it.

Our next home was in a little spa town called Bad Aussee. We arrived on a beautiful sunny day and all the people in the town came out to greet us. The main road was lined with people waving swastika flags and they clapped and cheered and Hail Hitlered as we drove past.

Bad Aussee seemed like a toy town. Nothing had been blitzed or damaged. The houses were brightly painted white and blue and yellow: large square town houses; tall hotels for the visitors who came to take the waters; churches with huge pointed steeples matching the huge pointed mountains all around. Everything could have been in one of Helmut's drawings. There was a great big river running through the middle of the town and our new Nanny, Rosi, took us for walks beside it to feed the ducks. Not that we had much food to spare for the ducks. We were back on rations, but much happier than at the Goerings'. Papa visited us for a couple of days and when he and Mummy left, the little ones clung to him. He called them limpets. I was the only one who managed not to cry. Papa said he was very proud of me for being so grown-up.

Day Six in the Bunker
Friday 27 April, 1945

Waking up is like dropping a stone. For a split second I have nothing more than a vague sense of being me and then I remember where we are. Check the shadows. Check the sounds. Can I hear Russian voices? How loud are the guns? Is the ventilation working?

Then there's always the question of whether or not to turn on the light to find out the time. I don't do it because it could still be the middle of the night and I don't want to wake up all the others. So I hold tight and wait and wait and wait for the sound of Mrs. Junge's quick, light steps.

We got dressed quite quietly today by our standards. No running around or larking from Heide or Helmut.

Porridge for breakfast. I tried to get away with just pushing it around the bowl but Mrs. Junge noticed, so

I pulled myself together and put a small spoonful of the ugly grey lumps into my mouth and I have to admit it wasn't as bad as I expected. A bit watery, but I added a ton of sugar and it was actually alright. It's nice that we can have as much sugar as we like here.

After breakfast Papa came up from the Leader Bunker and gave us all a pat on the head. He told us two jokes. "How many gears on a Russian tank? Four: one forward, three reverse." "Why do French tanks have rear view mirrors? So that they can watch the battle." They made Helmut laugh.

Papa repeated his little speech about how we are an example to all Germans because we are showing our loyalty to the Leader at this dark hour. History will remember us and respect our bravery. He says he announced all this to the German people on the radio. Then he was off, back down to the Leader Bunker to shut himself up with his secretary, Mr. Naumann. Mr. Naumann never comes up to our bunker, which is strange considering he's been Mummy's "rock" and living with us for most of the last year.

Liesl came to tidy our room so I went in to chat to her. She likes to get the bedcovers completely flat and once she's satisfied that every wrinkle has been removed she gives the bed a little pat of congratulation before moving on to the next one. When she was done she sat down on one of the lower bunks and I sat on the floor in front of her so she could brush out both my plaits and make new ones. I asked her what she thought was going to happen. She thinks it's still possible to get out, but she says that Uncle Leader has to stay and guard the capital, and Auntie Eva has to stay and look after Uncle Leader, and she has to stay and look after Auntie Eva. I told her Papa said we had to stay to show our loyalty to the Leader, and she nodded.

"Can Auntie Eva help you get news from Peter? Surely she could find out from one of the generals where his regiment is?"

"Oh no. I wouldn't bother Auntie Eva with my worries. She has enough troubles of her own."

"Really? She always seems so bright."

"She tries very hard to keep cheerful and to keep the Leader happy."

"Mummy says that's our job too. Do you want to have children one day, Liesl?"

"Definitely. I'd like to have four."

"Really? I only want two. Children are a lot of work."

Liesl laughed, "You have an old head on your young shoulders."

"Where will you and Peter live when you're married?"

"There's a little cottage on my parents' farm, and I hope we can live there. I'll be able to help my parents on the farm and Peter will be able to cycle to the shop."

"What will you do on the farm?"

"Lots of things. Milking, feeding the animals, helping Mother bottle and pickle. My brothers do most of the heavy work."

"How many brothers do you have?"

"Two – Hans and Max."

"Older or younger?"

"Both older."

"Are they married?"

"No."

"So they still live at home?"

"Well. They did. Max is in England now."

"England?"

"He was captured by the English."

"So was my brother Harald. Mummy says it's the best thing that can happen. She knows he'll be safe now."

Liesl nodded.

"What about Hans?"

Liesl shook her head. "We don't know."

I leant back on Liesl and she rocked me in her arms. It was so nice to be held and feel protected. We stayed like that until Heide burst in, looking for somewhere to hide.

I wasn't in the mood for hide-and-seek so I went down the steps to the Leader Bunker to look for the puppies. Mummy and Auntie Eva were in the corridor with Mrs. Junge. They were talking to one of the soldiers. The young one – about my age, maybe a bit older.

Very, very short hair, almost shaved. He was covered in dust. His uniform, his boots, his head, his face – everything was completely grey apart from his dark eyes. Auntie Eva was taking a handkerchief out of her pocket and giving it to him. He wiped his face with it, but only managed to smear the dirt around a bit. Then she poured him a glass of water from the jug on the trolley, and as he took it from her hand, he dropped it straight on the floor and it shattered. Auntie Eva poured him another one. She dipped her hanky in the water and wiped gently all around his eyes. "Calm down, calm down," she kept saying, kindly, as if she was talking to a dog. I don't think Mummy really noticed the boy, or me. She had one hand on her forehead as if she had a headache. I think she even had her eyes closed. I couldn't stop watching. Auntie Eva called an orderly to clear up the broken glass. And then the boy rushed off. I hope I see him again.

Auntie Eva saw me on the stairs and gave me a huge smile. "I know what you're after – come with me and I'll show you!" All the puppies were asleep on her bed. I lay down and cuddled up with them, and as they woke up they all started wriggling and fidgeting and flopping on top of each other. I stroked Foxl behind his ears, which he loves. Auntie Eva was repairing her make-up when Mrs. Junge came in, all hurried and worried, and not waiting to see whether she was interrupting, which is unusual for her.

"The Leader is looking for Upper Group Leader Fegelein."

Auntie Eva looked confused, "Hermann? I have no idea. I don't think I've seen him for a few days. What is it about? Is there news from Gretl?"

"I – I'm not sure. I think you had better come."

Auntie Eva left me with the puppies. It sounds like Uncle Leader might have got a message that Auntie Eva's sister Gretl has had her baby.

I wasn't on my own for long because the others gave up playing hide-and-seek and came to see the puppies too. Mrs. Junge came back – much calmer this time – and called us for lunch. She wouldn't say what had happened so I still don't know whether Auntie Eva has a new niece or nephew.

Lunch was OK. Mashed potatoes and fried eggs. Then we went to lie down on our bunks and Hilde read the story of Snow White out loud. Helmut had the idea of us doing a Snow White play, with lots of dwarf yodelling. We agreed to give it a go, so long as he didn't get silly. I was Snow White, Hilde was the Wicked Queen and all the others were dwarves, with Helmut doubling as the Prince. I did a fantastic dying scene, I thought, when I was poisoned – clutching my throat and bulging my eyes. All the little dwarves wept loudly. Very dramatic. We practised it through twice and decided to do a performance for the grown-ups. We planned to do it at teatime, but no one came to get us ready, so, when my watch said four o'clock, we went out to see what was happening.

There were just the usual soldiers in the corridor. Mummy's door was closed. We went down the stairs to the Leader Bunker to see if we could find Mrs. Junge or Auntie Eva or Liesl.

We heard a door slam. Someone was shouting. We crouched down on the stairs to try to find out what was going on without being seen. Papa and Uncle Leader and Mr. Bormann came into the Leader Bunker corridor.

They were walking backwards and forwards, Uncle Leader at the front, shouting furiously. He was waving a big, torn piece of paper – a map, I think. In the end he flung it on the floor. Papa looked white, but Mr. Bormann just looked like he always does – so tightly stuffed into his suit he can hardly speak, very slightly swaying. You can never tell what he's thinking. The opposite of Papa – you can always tell how he's feeling from his face. Uncle Leader was yelling, "The traitors! The cowards!" He was bright red. We managed to crawl back up the stairs without anyone noticing us. Miss Manziarly was just setting out cakes and hot chocolate in the corridor of the Upper Bunker.

She said Uncle Leader was too busy for tea today. Clearly. So, no three-part harmony performance and no Snow White. We ate our tea in silence and listened out for more door slamming and shouting, but everything had gone quiet.

We didn't really know what to do at the end of tea. We had another rehearsal, but everyone was grumpy. Helmut kept spoiling it by laughing when I was dying. And then Hilde got upset and said that she wanted to be Snow White and she didn't want to be the Wicked Queen, so we gave up and decided to go and find the puppies. Again.

The Leader Bunker corridor was empty. The puppies weren't in their little room, so we went to see whether they were in Auntie Eva's. We were just about to knock when we heard loud crying. We ran as fast as we could back up the stairs to the Upper Bunker. I don't know what's going on. I'm pretty sure it was Auntie Eva crying. It could be something to do with Gretl's baby – or it could be to do with Uncle Leader being so angry.

When we got back upstairs Mummy was looking for us. She took us into our bedroom.

"Listen carefully, children. I need to tell you something important. Sit down, Heide."

For a moment I thought she was going to explain what was going on.

"Now I'm very proud of all of you. You've all been really good children and not made any fuss at all. You are proper little soldiers. And because we're all living like soldiers we're going to need to have a special injection which soldiers have to keep them strong."

"Why?"

"Well, we're living with lots of people down here and if someone got an illness it could spread very quickly, so we all need to have this injection to protect us from getting sick.

"I'm going to go to see Dr. Kunz this evening to arrange for him to come and give you your injections. Mrs. Junge is also going to be busy this evening because Uncle Leader has got lots of typing for her to do. We have arranged for one of the nurses, Miss Flegel, to put you to bed. She's very nice and I know you'll all be good and help each other and not give her any trouble."

"Mummy, when can we show you our play?" Holde asked.

"I'm not sure, darling. Everyone's very busy at the moment. This is a very important time."

"Is the war going to end soon?" Helmut asked.

"Yes, very soon. And we've all got to be good and brave."

I'm a bit confused about why we need the injection if the war's going to end soon.

Miss Flegel was alright, though I didn't like the look of her. She has a completely square face and dark hair tied back flat. She's been nursing General von Greim and she said that his leg – apparently it's not just his foot that was hurt but all the lower part of that leg too – will get better. She says that we have the world's top doctors here in the bunker. She got us to sing the song that Hanna Reitsch had taught us and then turned out the light and sang until all the little ones were asleep. She sang the lullaby Granny used to sing to us:

Sleep, sleep, in the sweet grave,
Your mother's arm protects you.
All you dream of and all you have
She keeps warm with her love.

Sleep, sleep, in the lap of the land
The sounds of love surround you
A lily, a rose,
Will be yours when you wake.

After she'd gone I tried to talk to Hilde, but she's a million miles away from me. She said that she just wanted to sleep. She sucked in her cheeks and turned to face the wall. I thought I could hear her crying but it was hard to be sure through all the rattling shells. She just pulled the blankets over her head and told me to shut up. She always has to make things as bad as they can be. Bite off her nose to spite her face. And there's never anything I can do.

I tried to think about Liesl in her cottage with her little brood of children. Then I heard the music. Only in snatches, filling the silences between the shells. Thumping feet and wailing violins. Someone, somewhere must have been having a party. I asked Hilde if she could hear it, but she didn't reply. She may have been asleep. I finally drifted off to the music and the shelling and dreams of the dusty soldier boy.

The summer when I was ten we made a film for Papa. It was Mummy's idea. We spent the summer in the countryside, away from the bombing – Swan Island, then Castle Lanke, and finally a farm in the small village of Obergau. Papa had to stay in Berlin because of work. We wanted him to be able to see the fatherland in all its summer glory.

It was quite good fun making the film because we did lots of nice things – swimming, riding, playing with the farm animals, picnicking in the woods – so that we could get them on the film. At one point we filmed a visit from General Field Marshall Rommel. He's my favourite general. We lined up on the front steps and presented him with flowers when he arrived. We were all on our best behaviour, even Heide, who didn't always put on her best front for filming. In fact, the film begins with Heide complaining about Papa hurting her bottom when he smacked her, which I thought we should cut out, but Mummy said Papa would think that was funny. Mummy says Papa likes to see a bit of spirit. I hate that about grown-ups. They drum it into you that you've got to be good and not make a fuss and you try your hardest to do that, only to discover that they think your little sister is really sweet when she behaves like a rascal.

I had my birthday during the filming and we filmed

Mummy giving me an accordion and me playing it really badly. That's the most embarrassing bit – at least as far as I'm concerned. The film ends, as the summer ended, at school in Wandlitz. They filmed Helmut in his class.

It started with the "Hail Hitler" salute.

"Today," said the teacher, "I am feeling really curious. I would like to know what you children would like to be when you grow up." The teacher himself was more than grown up – one of those who had been brought out of retirement because so many teachers had joined the army. He was thin, bald, with a shorn halo of white hair.

Almost all the hands in the class shot up. Helmut was chosen. He stands very properly, hands straight down by his sides. Papa will like that.

"I would like to be a forester."

"I would like that too," says the teacher. Helmut sits back down and the teacher picks other children. He only chooses boys. Another one wants to be a forester. Someone wants to be a hunter.

At last he chooses a girl, "Margaret."

She stands up with a big smile, "A nurse."

"A good job for a woman. Some jobs are right for girls, some for boys. Look at all these hands. I can't ask all of you. Helmut, tell us, why do you want to be a forester?"

Helmut jumps back out of his seat. This time he

stutters. "Because I like being with animals and being in the beautiful forest."

"Yes, being a forester is a good healthy job. What skills do you need to be a forester?"

Again, he picks on the boys to answer. Someone mentions shooting, someone mentions maths.

"Indeed. I have a friend who is a forester. He shoots ducks. There are ten ducks. He shoots one, how many are left?"

Almost everyone's hand goes up, but not Helmut's.

"Helmut?"

Helmut jumps back up. He hasn't been listening. He stutters more, "The same number as before, minus one."

"And how many is that?"

Silence from Helmut; he looks all round the room. Hands sticking up and waving all around.

"How many were there before?"

Long pause, "Seven?"

"Try again."

Someone must have muttered it.

"Ten."

"Correct, and how many were shot?"

"One."

"Correct, so how many are left?"

You can see the relief on Helmut's face – he thinks he is on safe ground: "Ten minus one is nine, so nine ducks are left."

"No. There are none left. Who can explain why there are none left?"

This time he actually chooses a girl.

"So, Helmut," he says, "having heard her explanation. Tell us all why there are no ducks left."

"Because," Helmut stammers, repeating the girl's words, "the ducks have been scared by the shot and they have all flown away!"

Granny B. was with us all summer. If I couldn't sleep I would go down in the evenings and she would ask one of the maids to make us warm milk and we would sit on the sofa – she would be doing her embroidery and I would be knitting – and she would tell me all her stories about the olden days, picking up from wherever she felt like, depending on what mood she was in.

"Of course, your mother's marriage to Gunther Quandt didn't last. The age difference was too great. But I think the thing that finally ended it was her stepson Helmut's death. It devastated your mother. He was only eighteen. He had appendicitis. He should not have died but he was studying, first in London and then in Paris, and the stupid, stupid English and French doctors didn't know what they were doing. In London they told him to avoid spicy foods and to sleep with a hot-water bottle. He just got iller and iller. Finally a French doctor diagnosed his problem and operated, but it was too late, the appendix had burst and the poison had spread throughout his body. Magda and Gunther rushed from Berlin. He was in agonies. Not even morphine could help him. Magda stayed with him for three days. He died in her arms, whilst Gunther paced up and down the streets. I don't think they ever spoke about it. It was like a wound at the heart of their marriage. Something too painful to touch. Two years later they divorced, and to be fair, Gunther was generous to her, and he has always been a good father to Harald. He allowed Harald to live with her, unless she remarried, which of course she did, when she married your father. Harald must have been about ten. But even then Gunther made sure that Harald was living so close to his mother that, in fact, he spent most of his time with her."

"What happened to Mummy's friend Victor?"

"Well, he followed his dream, and he died for it. He went to live in the new Jewish homeland in Palestine and became one of the chief negotiators, I believe, with the British and German governments. But one evening he was strolling on the beach with his wife when two men approached. The story goes that they came up to Victor and asked him the time. As he reached for his pocket watch one of the men shot him. There were memorial services for him in four different countries – you would have been a baby at this time – the Berlin memorial service was held in the Philharmonie Hall. It was enormous. Thousands must have attended. There were certainly reports of hundreds of people crowding the streets outside. That will have been a comfort to his mother. Of course, your mother couldn't go – it wouldn't be done for the wife of Josef Goebbels to be seen at the funeral of a Jew. Not after all the trouble there had been with the Jewish Question. I imagine she had her memories."

I always wanted to hear about when Mummy and Papa met.

"Well, they're the ones to ask about that. All I know is that after the divorce your mother was looking for something to keep her busy. All the talk was of the Nazis – how they were going to turn this country around, and one of her friends took her to a rally. That's where she first saw your father. I remember meeting her in a café shortly after. She told me of her plans to volunteer to work in your father's office.

"'Mama,' she said. 'You have never seen anything like it. The energy. The intelligence. This man is electric. He is going to set Germany on fire.'

"She's always liked powerful men, your mother, always. I wonder whether you will be the same."

❧

The year ended with one of our most miserable Christmases. It started with a visit to see Mummy in the sanatorium. It was about two weeks before Christmas, and we were supposed to be celebrating Mummy and Papa's wedding anniversary. Mummy was recovering from a heart attack. She looked old without her make-up on, and she had big black bags under her eyes. We took bunches of ivy and laurel because we didn't have any flowers in the garden.

We'd planned to sing her some carols but she had a bad headache, so we sang her a very quiet lullaby:

Do you know how many little stars there are
Up in heaven's blue tent?
Do you know how many clouds wander
Far across the world?
The Lord God has counted them all
Not a single one is missing
Out of the whole big number.

We thought she'd be home for Christmas, but she wasn't well enough. It meant we didn't wrap the presents for the poor, which is one of my best bits. I always help by holding down the paper whilst Mummy ties the ribbons, and the dining room always feels so cosy with the fire blazing and the lamps shining and all the beautiful wrapping paper laid out on the table. The scissors are always lost and my legs get pins and needles, but at the end of the afternoon we have two big piles of presents – one for the poor and one for the servants.

This year the piles just appeared ready wrapped. I think Papa's secretaries must have done them. We still went to the big party to give out the presents but it just didn't feel Christmassy.

It was the same with decorating the tree on Christmas Eve. The maids did it instead of Mummy and it didn't feel at all exciting. Because of rationing, all the decorations were wooden and metal; nothing you could eat, no little marzipan apples. Papa read us the Christmas story and we opened our presents – I can't remember what they were – and we munched little bits of chopped-up apple and some raisins instead of chocolate. I knew Edda Goering would be stuffing her ugly little face with all the chocolates and marzipan she could shovel in. We tried to persuade Papa to let us have a little bit of chocolate for Christmas, but he insisted that we couldn't: "We must show the servants a good example. We are not the Goerings. We are not cheats."

I am proud of Mummy and Papa, but sometimes I wish our parents weren't such goody-goodies, always doing what's right rather than what's nice.

Day Seven in the Bunker
Saturday 28 April, 1945

Tea with Uncle Adi was very crowded: Auntie Eva, Mummy and Papa, Flight Captain Reitsch, General Von Greim, all the dogs. Uncle Leader's mind was completely elsewhere. He didn't play with Blondi or do any tricks. He didn't ask any questions. He just ate cake. His hand was shakier than ever. He spilled his hot chocolate again, all down the front of his jacket, but this time he either didn't notice or he didn't care. He stuffed the cake into his mouth. Crumbs stuck to his moustache. The room smells revolting.

Flight Captain Reitsch did most of the talking. How brave the German soldiers are. What a beautiful spring. I don't know. Anyway, in the end she did what I was dreading and clapped her hands:

"My Leader, I have taught the children a new song which they are going to sing for you."

Uncle Adi shifted his position on the sofa and picked up another piece of cake.

"Children." She fixed her staring eyes upon us.

We got into our positions in a semi circle facing Uncle Adi. Flight Captain Reitsch stood with her back to him conducting us, and blocking my view of him, so I had no idea whether he was enjoying it.

We sang the lullaby through, once all together and then in two parts – me and Heide and Helmut together, Hilde and Holde and Hedda together – and then in three parts. I was with Heide. I expected to find Uncle Adi snoozing by the time we finished, but he clapped one hand on his knee with mild enthusiasm.

All the other grown-ups clapped loudly, and then everyone went quiet. None of us mentioned Snow White. Not even Helmut. Auntie Eva suggested that we go and play hide-and-seek. And that was that.

<hr />

All these days are blurring into one. I'm playing patience. Mummy strokes my hair as she wafts past. Smiles vaguely, but doesn't look me in the eye. Mrs. Junge twitters endlessly but doesn't say anything useful, and she doesn't stop and listen if you ask her a question. Papa either doesn't notice us at all, if we see him in the Leader Bunker, or he comes up here and claps his hands and asks how everyone is, and is all smiles for a moment, and then he's gone. Every time he tells us the

135

same thing: "We're very close to victory now. The troops are fighting magnificently." I used to believe him, but now I can see that his eyes are lying. He doesn't believe it himself. The others haven't a clue. Helmut always says "Hurray!" None of them worry about the war at all.

It must have been this morning that I saw Auntie Eva talking to Mrs. Junge and one of the other secretaries – a woman called Dara; I don't really know her. Liesl says she was a model for Elizabeth Arden before she came to work for Uncle Leader. She's quite beautiful in a slightly horsey way. Auntie Eva became quite giggly and in a loud whisper – which us children could obviously hear, but we knew we were meant to pretend that we couldn't – she said to the two secretaries: "I bet you'll be crying again by this evening."

Mrs. Junge looked horrified. "Will it be as soon as that?" Dara was sucking hard on her cigarette.

But Auntie Eva was laughing. "No, not like that. It's nothing to worry about. I can't tell you any more about it yet."

The thing that bothered me about this conversation was not Auntie Eva's secretiveness, which is really no surprise, but Mrs. Junge's reaction. She's clearly expecting something very bad to happen.

I asked Auntie Eva whether Gretl had had her baby, but she said she didn't know. So I've no idea what yesterday's crying was all about.

Mummy put us to bed tonight. She read us "The Wolf and the Man" from the Brothers Grimm book; it's one of the shortest but quite funny. The she clapped the book shut and, giving each of us a quick kiss on the forehead, flicked off the light switch and left. In the dark with my eyes shut I can see the young soldier boy dropping the glass, and I can see it shatter on the concrete floor.

Mummy took me and Hilde to the Sport Palace where Papa was making a very important speech. There were hundreds and hundreds of rows of people, hats on laps. Papa was amazing. The whole crowd screamed and cheered. His message was that every single German had to put all their effort into the war. This is total war. Everyone has to be involved. We need one million more soldiers and we can easily find them. Everything which doesn't contribute to the war effort is going to be closed down: there will be no more circuses, no more theatres, no more restaurants, no more shops except chemists, grocers and cobblers. And the grocers will have to sell essential food, no fancy stuff. Cake-making is banned. Women have got to do all the jobs they possibly can so that all men are free to join the army. For instance, only women are going to be allowed to cut hair, even men's hair. All the barbers have got to join the army. Grandmothers will have to look after the children so that all women under 50 can do useful jobs. And everyone has to make do without servants so that the servants can help us win the war too.

Sitting in the car on the way home, I was trying to imagine what it was going to be like, but Mummy said that for us nothing much was going to change. I felt rather disappointed. She said that because she and Papa are already working so hard for the war effort, and for the German people, they really couldn't manage so many children and houses without servants. Uncle Leader has made Papa Empire Plenipotentiary for Total Mobilisation, which means he's in charge of everything really now – not just films and newspapers. It's a great honour. And Mummy is taking on even more war work. She is going to work for a factory, sewing uniforms, although she's going to do the sewing on her own machine at Castle Lanke, then each week she'll take the things she's made into the factory. At work Papa has had to close lots of departments. For instance, they've had to give up making cartoons. Papa says that once we've won the war we'll go full speed ahead on cartoons and soon be making even better ones than the Americans. Colour ones.

In his speech, Papa explained that the Russian Communists are trying to take over the whole of Europe. They want a Jewish World Revolution. Unless we stop them the Russians will overtake Germany and then the Jewish murder squads will come in and kill all the leaders, all the intelligent people. Papa says a family like ours would be one of the first to be killed, which actually might be quite lucky for us because everyone else will be forced into slavery and millions will die of starvation. England should be helping us fight against this evil, but they are being stupid. Papa says they have been tricked into thinking that Jews are perfectly safe. So it's up to us Germans to save Europe.

There were lots of wounded soldiers at the front of the stadium. Hilde and I saw one man who had lost an arm and he was clapping his leg like mad with his good hand. We tried it to see if you could make as loud a noise with one hand as you can with two, but Mummy said it was rude to copy.

Papa was shouting so much and thumping the air that he was completely dripping with sweat. At the end of the speech he shouted: "Now people arise and let the storm break loose!" And everybody went absolutely mad, cheering the Leader and clapping and doing the Hail Victory salute. It was crazy, and then somehow we all started singing *Germany, Germany, above all, above all the world!*, which always makes the hair on my arms stand on end. Thousands of people all singing at the tops of their voices. It felt like the whole nation was joined together: and no one could defeat us! I felt so proud of Papa.

❧

This was one of the best years of the war because we stayed in one place – Castle Lanke – most of the time and went to school in Wandlitz. Things began to feel a bit more normal, and more like we were in our own home, which is much better than feeling like you're a guest all the time. We also got another new nanny – well, she wasn't really a nanny – we were too old for a nanny – she was a governess. The youngest three had their own governess, Miss Schroeter, who was as old as the hills, but Hilde and Helmut and I had Hubi –Miss Hubner, but we called her Hubi, even after she married and became Mrs. Leske. She mostly helped Helmut with catch-up lessons because he tended to get behind at school. At first I didn't like her because I didn't need extra help and I didn't want to do extra work. Also Helmut seemed to be her favourite. She called him "little brother" because he had the same birthday as her brother, which was annoying, but actually she turned out to be very kind and good at sticking up for us.

Mostly Papa wasn't there, because he had to stay in Berlin and work, but sometimes he came home at weekends. As soon as he walked through the door it was like someone had switched a bright light on. Instead of quietly eating our meals, telling Mummy about school and concentrating on spreading our butter ration as far as possible, suddenly there was no time to think about what you were eating because Papa was blasting questions:

"What's the capital of Japan?"

"Name three operas by Wagner."

"Name five other German composers."

"13 x 13?"

"Quick, quick, quick. Come on Helmut – don't let your sisters show you up!"

And then there were games. Games you never knew whether to win or lose, because Papa likes to see us do our best, but sometimes he bites our heads off if he loses.

Chase around the table was one game. It was easy to win because we could duck under the table and Papa couldn't – normally that was fine. In the end, or actually quite quickly, Papa would catch Heide and tickle her and we'd all laugh. But one day Helmut, who was trying to make up for not knowing the name of the leader of Russia, even though I was mouthing it across the table, decided to prove his ability by sticking a hand out from under the table and grabbing at Papa's ankle as he ran past. Papa went flying, knocking over a side table. We all stopped dead. Papa went bright red and the sides of his jaws started throbbing, which is always a bad sign. I went over to help him get up, but he screamed at me to get away. We all backed out of the room as quickly as we could, even Papa's adjutants Schwagermann and von Oven. Papa started yelling for Helmut. Bravely, Helmut went back into the room on his own. We could hear Papa shouting and shouting about what an idiot Helmut was, what a disappointment. It went on and on. The rest of the house was silent. Eventually Helmut emerged, his face deep red and smeared with tears. He rushed straight up to his room, slamming the door behind him. We all left him alone to get over it. About half an hour later, Papa called for Hubi.

When Papa had been shouting at Helmut, Hubi had

muttered under her breath, "That man's a sadist." I didn't know what a sadist was, and it wasn't a time to ask questions, but apparently one of the kitchen staff reported her to Papa for insulting him.

Hubi was in Papa's office for ages. We thought she was going to get the sack, but in the end she came out quite calmly and went up to see Helmut. Having heard Papa shouting for Hubi, he was now more worried that he would lose Hubi than upset about being told off by Papa. She told Helmut that Papa was a fair man who could see when he made a mistake, and there would be no more punishments.

I think it was after the tripping incident that Mummy and Papa got Georg Schertz to come and stay to be a friend for Helmut. They decided he needed someone other than Papa to trip up, and that being with all us girls the whole time was turning him into a sissy. I heard Hubi telling Cook. They chose Georg because he came from a good family with a house on Swan Island. Georg was OK. Quite shy, and he didn't stop being shy even though he stayed with us at Castle Lanke for most of a summer. He never talked much to anyone except Helmut. Actually, to be strictly truthful, I don't think he talked much to Helmut. They just endlessly arrested each other and spied on each other and shot each other with sticks.

The only time the rest of us saw friends was at school. The teacher, Mr. Klink, was a bit strict. He was very old, with little round glasses and fluffy white hair. Like all my teachers, he always picked boys to answer the questions. Often I'd have my hand up so long it felt like it was going to drop off and I'd have to prop it up with my other hand. I don't think he thought there was much point in teaching girls. He'd ask us questions which we had to chant the answers to:

"What is the most noble life?"

"The life of a farmer is the most noble life."

"What is a woman's greatest destiny?"

"A woman's greatest destiny is to be a mother."

He'd come back from retirement and he had loads of stories about the last war. He'd fought in France. He told us about the mud and the rats and endless rattle of the artillery. He told us about the treachery of the Jews, stealing the soldiers' money. He told us about his friend Fritz who was killed by a grenade as he passed Mr. Klink a cigarette. His stories made the class very quiet. Most of the children were thinking of their fathers at the front.

My two best friends were Anni and Sophie. I liked Anni the minute I met her because she had curly black hair and thick black eyelashes that made you stare at her eyes. Anni and her twin brother Rudi had come to Wandlitz to live with their grandmother after their house in Berlin was bombed. Sophie told me that Anni's mother and baby brother were killed, but Anni never talked about that. Sophie told me stories about all the children. Whose father had been killed, or was missing. She had lived her whole life in Wandlitz and seemed to know everything about everything. She didn't have any brothers or sisters and she lived alone with her mother. You could tell. She had neat plaits and a well-stocked pencil case. And if I played too much with Anni she would pretend to ignore us until one of us went and begged her to join in. I didn't think about it at the time, but the one person she never talked about was her own father. I really felt I could trust Anni and Sophie because they never teased me about being a Goebbels. Helmut had to put up with a lot of that. There was a group of boys in his class who did exaggerated limps in the playground and apparently they had this mad staring-eye look that they'd give each other when Helmut spoke in class.

Both our grannies had houses in the grounds of Castle Lanke. Every Sunday afternoon we would go and visit Granny Goebbels and sing to her. Always when we got there she'd be sitting in her chair with her eyes closed, muttering to herself and fingering her rosary beads. Papa didn't usually come with us, but she would always ask after him. She used to call him "that boy" as if she didn't realise that he had grown up. "What has that boy done now?" she would ask. "Always up to no good. I don't know how many grey hairs he's given me!" A lot, was the answer: her hair was completely white. Every Sunday she said the same things. And Auntie Maria who was living with her always said, "Come on, Mother, you know what he's like." And she'd say "I know, I know, I know – that's why I spend so much time praying for his soul!"

It upset her that Papa wouldn't go to church with her. She had great big odd-shaped knuckles, and if she wasn't fiddling with her beads she would be rubbing her knuckles. Her hands were never still. When we were little she used to make us lots of itchy cardigans and jumpers, but now she complained that she couldn't knit like she used to. Papa had this joke that it was because of Granny Goebbels' sore knuckles that we were winning the war. He said that the real reason we lost the last war was because she had sent so many itchy socks to the front that the soldiers were driven crazy by their itchy legs. This war she couldn't knit and the soldiers could concentrate on fighting without the distraction of her itchy socks.

Granny Goebbels was too stiff to come over to the Castle, but when Mummy was home Granny B. usually came over in the evening to play cards. They would often end up arguing. We could hear them from the nursery. Mummy's voice would be like a low rumble of thunder; we could never hear her actual words, and then Granny B. would shriek like lightning: "You have ruined all our lives!" or "You should never have married that evil little man!"

It was in Castle Lanke that I really realised how much Granny B. and Papa hated each other. I noticed that she never visited when Papa was home, but she had a habit of leaving things behind in the house – her shawl, her glasses, her tablets, her sewing – and when Papa got back from Berlin he would immediately spot these things and it would drive him mad. He would order them to be taken straight back to her lodge: "Look what the old bat's left behind this time." And Mummy would say "Josef!" in a you-shouldn't-say-that-but-I-know-what-you-mean tone.

Day Eight in the Bunker
Sunday 29 April, 1945

I asked Mrs. Junge about the music the other night and she said there'd been a wedding in the cellars of the Empire Chancellery. One of the kitchen maids married one of the drivers. They danced to the music of a small group of SS musicians playing Gypsy wedding songs. There always used to be Gypsy bands at weddings. It is supposed to bring good luck to the marriage. Papa's sister, Auntie Maria, had a Gypsy band at her wedding. There were four of them, all wearing big white shirts and tall leather boots which they stamped in time to the music. The violins started mournfully and slowly, but they gradually got faster and faster, and this great stamping rhythm kicked in. Hilde and I held hands and swung out our bodies, whirling and whirling, until we fell on top of each other in a laughing sweaty heap. I haven't seen any Gypsy bands since the war started. People like Hubi have just been having very simple weddings, without the big parties. It will be so lovely when we can whirl and celebrate again. I heard some more music last night, but it was quieter. Thin, faint, ghost music. Violin and accordion, I think. Maybe another wedding, but smaller.

It feels like everyone has left. The corridors are emptier. I've been looking out for Upper Group Leader Fegelein to ask him about Gretl's baby, but I haven't seen him for days. And even the people who are here seem somehow absent. No one looks you in the eye. Nothing seems real.

I've been looking out for the soldier boy but I haven't seen him either.

Liesl did my plaits again. I asked her what she thought happened when we die.

"We go to heaven."

"Do you really believe that? Mummy believes in reincarnation. She says that we have lots of lives. If we lead a good life and die an honourable death, we will have an even better life next time."

"Uh-ha. What kind of life would you choose next time?"

"Maybe I'd be a Red Indian brave and ride bareback across the plains. What about you?"

"I'd like a peaceful life. I wouldn't mind where, so long as there was no war. I wouldn't mind being a tree, so long as no one cut me down."

"Do you think we can get out of here without being killed?"

She rubbed her eyes. She's got that sort of soft loose skin that rolls under your fingers when you rub it.

"We're all hoping that the Russians will surrender very soon."

"But what if they don't? I'm sure that the sound of the guns is getting louder, which means that they're getting closer. How are we going to get out of here before it's too late?"

"Helga, my lovely, I don't know. We will just have to see, and when the time comes to get out of here, whether the Russians have surrendered or not, I will do all I can to help you."

"You won't go without us?"

"I won't go without you."

I lay my head back on her shoulder and she put her arm around me.

We were awake for ages this morning before anyone came to get us. Again I was woken by ceiling dust on my face. Hedda and Heide were already up with the light on, dancing in a circle and singing:

Ring a ring a roses
Sugar in the pot
Lard in the tub

Tomorrow we will fast
The day after tomorrow we'll slaughter the lamb
And it will cry: baah!

In the end we were really hungry and got ourselves dressed. It was ten according to the clock on the wall. We went to the kitchen and one of the orderlies gave us some bread and jam. There was a strange smell coming from the Leader Bunker. A bit like marzipan, but very bitter; it caught the back of your throat. Put us off our breakfast.

In the end Mummy appeared. She explained that all the grown-ups were very tired because Auntie Eva and Uncle Adi had got married in the middle of the night! So that's what the music was, and Auntie Eva's mysterious comment. We wanted to go and see Auntie Eva after breakfast, but of course she was still asleep, so we didn't see her till teatime.

I asked Mummy about the smell. She said that she had no idea what it was and, anyway, it wasn't polite to talk about smells.

We thought today would be a good day to do our Snow White performance, as a kind of wedding present. We rehearsed during our afternoon rest. It went quite well. No rows. However, tea turned out to be the most dismal yet. No play, but worse than that, no puppies. They didn't even give us a chance to say goodbye to them.

Auntie Eva was twizzling her new ring. "I'm so sorry, darlings. You know this isn't a good place for little puppies to grow up. They need lots of space and they need to be able to play outside. It's not natural for dogs to be living underground like this. We've sent them to Berchtesgaden. They'll be much happier. I know we'll all miss them rotten, but I'm afraid in war we all have to make sacrifices and it won't be long until we are all out of here and we'll see them again."

Helmut asked what we were all thinking. "Can we go to Berchtesgaden too?"

"Of course, my darlings. Uncle Leader would love that. We'll all go there as soon as this horrible war is over."

He meant now. Obviously. But we didn't say anything else. There isn't any point. I had a horrible closed feeling in the back of my mouth. I knew that if I opened my lips to speak I wouldn't be able to stop myself crying. I don't know why grown-ups think that if they don't tell you about something then you won't be upset by it.

What I wanted to know was how they got the dogs out. Flight Captain Reitsch and General von Greim have gone too, but I'm sure they didn't take the dogs because Auntie Eva said that they flew off in the middle of the night. We didn't get to say goodbye to them either. Apparently Uncle Adi has given them some special secret mission. I know the puppies were definitely still here in the morning, because I can remember hearing them barking when I was playing patience. I'm furious that I was playing stupid patience, when I could have been cuddling Foxl.

Helmut had to try really hard not to cry but I don't think that any of the grown-ups noticed. I forget that he does really mind about things, because he's always pretending to be tough. We all felt too sad to suggest doing Snow White. None of the grown-ups said much. They perched quietly, sipping their tea, except Uncle Adi, who slurped loudly and took disgusting big sips of tea into a mouth full of cake.

After tea, Papa and Mummy took us to a party in one of the cellars of the Empire Chancellery. It was to say thank you to all Papa's staff. Most of them are going to leave now. Mummy says it's different for them. No explanation.

There were salami sandwiches, cake, of course, and champagne for the grown-ups. I wasn't hungry. We sat around a table. One of the young soldiers sang old songs, mostly lullabies for some reason; I suppose that's all he could remember. Lots of people were crying, but silently, which is strange.

The party carried on after we'd gone to bed. I lay in bed listening to distant music, but this time it was from a gramophone.

The corridor outside our room is very noisy tonight too. Soldiers.

Personally I think we should save the celebrations until we've won the war.

1944

My memories have nearly caught up with me. Castle Lanke, the lawns, my birthday tea in the garden – milk and blackberries and the kind September sun.

Actually lots of bad things happened that year. Granny B. went mad. Not completely mad, but mad enough to be embarrassing: bursting into tears unexpectedly, making scenes. She would storm into the house, yelling for Mummy. I remember one afternoon – we'd just got back from school and were all in the hall taking off our coats – when she rushed in through the front door, looking half crazed with her grey hair tumbling out of its bun, screaming, "Where's your mother? Where's your mother?" Mummy came running through from her bedroom and swept Granny B. into the drawing room. We could hear her screaming at Mummy that she'd had enough and she was going to throw herself in the lake. She kept crying, "Why should I wait for a Russian bayonet?" Helmut thought she was saying, "Why should I wait for a Russian baronet?", which made us all giggle but we stopped pretty quickly when Mummy came out into the hall and shouted for help. Mr. Naumann came and took Granny by the arms and escorted her back to her lodge. Mr. Naumann helps Mummy with everything; he's taken over from Mr. Hanke.

Mummy came and went. Sometimes she was in

Berlin with Papa. Sometimes she was in the clinic in Dresden. Usually she went for treatment for her weak heart, but once because her face had frozen. It was really strange. She just woke up one day and she couldn't move half her face. She could only do a half-smile – the other side was stuck in a miserable droop. I remember her trying to eat breakfast and dribbling her coffee down her chin. She went off in one of the official cars later that morning and stayed in the Dresden clinic until it got better. I can't remember how long she was away, but even after her treatment I don't think her smile came back completely. She spent hours and hours walking round the big hall listening to the gramophone. She played the same song over and over again. It was from an opera which tells the story of Orpheus and Eurydice – the song Orpheus sings when he realises that he has lost Eurydice for ever. She played it at full volume so the sad music floated through the whole house.

It was when she came back from the clinic that I realised that there was some mystery about Harald. When he first went off to war he wrote us long letters and all six of us snuggled up on a sofa with Mummy and she would read them out. But there hadn't been a letter for ages. I asked Mummy if she'd had a letter in Dresden – maybe there was one we'd missed – or perhaps Papa had received one in Berlin. But she just shook her head in a "no", almost a twitch, clenching her neck so the thin bones at the front stood out.

Naps were her other big thing. She spent hours with her bedroom door shut and the curtains drawn, resting. And hours sitting in the yellow winged chair in her bedroom, reading the Buddhist books that Grandpa Ritschel had given her. We weren't to disturb her. I remember on her birthday we waited and waited for her to get up so that we could give her her presents. Hubi had helped us make things. I'd cross-stitched a handkerchief with a big "M" and we'd all picked flowers from the garden. We laid a beautiful breakfast table, but she didn't come down and she didn't come down. In the end Hubi said it would be alright to take her presents up to her bedroom. It was nearly lunchtime. We went in and Hubi pulled back the curtains and Mummy sat up against her pillows, covered up to her neck by the pale pink flowers of her eiderdown, sipping the coffee that Hubi had brought, and we sang her the birthday songs we'd been practising. It seemed strange that Mummy, with her big strong hands, had become so weak and delicate, while Hubi, with her skinny legs and round shoulders, was now the person who could cope with anything.

A happier memory is Hubi getting married. It was exciting even though we didn't get to go to her wedding and we were worried that it would mean that she would have her own children and leave us – we didn't know then that we would end up leaving her. We gave her a lamp with a china stand and a china shepherd and shepherdess holding hands. They were meant to represent her and Mr. Leske. He sometimes came to stay at Castle Lanke. He was very tall, so tall you got the feeling that he was a bit embarrassed to take up so much space.

Because we couldn't go to her wedding, Hubi put on her wedding dress to show us, and she looked really beautiful, though she would have looked even better if she didn't stoop forward so much, and personally I'd prefer a dress that went down to the ground, but you can't really have one like that in wartime. The dress was white but Hubi only had her normal black shoes to wear with it, which ruined the look, so Mummy said she could borrow a pair of her shoes, because they have the same size feet. We all went to Mummy's shoe cupboard to help her choose. She tried on about 50 pairs before she chose a really lovely grey silk pair with thin high heels, and she kept saying, "Oh Mrs. Goebbels, this is so kind of you! What if I spoil them? Oh Mrs. Goebbels!" But of course, she didn't spoil them.

❧❦❧

I only went to Berlin a couple of times in the whole year. Once was to go to the dentist and once to the military hospital.

Papa wanted to make a film of me and Hilde taking

flowers to wounded soldiers. We went in one of the official cars, and all the film people followed. The hospital was in an enormous building, surrounded by parks and gardens. It was a beautiful sunny day. There was a line of soldiers standing on the lawn to greet us. We all waited whilst the cameramen set up their cameras. Then we followed Papa, walking along the line, shaking hands.

It wasn't that easy. Several of them didn't have hands to shake. Three of them didn't have arms at all; some had lost their right arm, so had to shake with the left. Lots of them were on crutches – missing a leg – and so shaking hands was a bit of a balancing act. The ones who had no legs and were in wheelchairs were the easiest. We each had a bunch of flowers that we gave to the nurse standing at the end of the row, because she had the hands to hold them.

Then we went inside. Up big stone steps, through huge tall doors and into a vast pillared hall that stank of disinfectant. There was a team of white-coated doctors to take us on a tour of the wards. We set off down a long corridor, the doctors in front, the film crew behind, our shoes clattering on the brown and yellow floor tiles, the sun streaming through the big windows on one side.

There must have been about 100 beds in the ward. We started on the window side. Papa went first and introduced me and Hilde. We shook hands, as far as possible, smiled and moved on. It was very hot. Our light summer coats suddenly felt much too warm and heavy. There was a terrible smell, which the disinfectant failed to hide, that reminded me of the smell of the dead rat we found in the cellar at Castle Lanke. I started to feel sick. The whole room seemed to be groaning. We came to a man who had most of his face hidden by a bandage. He put out a hand to shake hands and Hilde took it without noticing that he had only got one finger. She didn't mean to scream, but that was it. "Switch off the cameras!" Papa swung out of the room. We had to run to keep up with him in the corridor.

Both me and Hilde had nightmares. Limping men stretching out mutilated hands. Mummy was furious with Papa for taking us there. I don't think they ever finished the film.

It was on a separate trip to Berlin that Hubi took me and Hilde to the dentist. I find it hard to remember the order in which things happened but I know exactly the date of our appointment because it became famous: the 20th of July.

I had to have a filling, which was agony. The dentist told me to make an elephant's mouth. He said I should raise my hand if it was too painful. Some people have gas, but he didn't think a brave girl like me would need gas. Hubi said I'd feel better afterwards if I didn't have gas and we were going to meet Papa for lunch. So I didn't have gas and I didn't lift my hand and the dentist screeched his drill into my tooth and it was hell. Hubi gave me a boiled sweet afterwards for being such a good girl and not making a fuss. I hadn't seen a boiled sweet for ages – I don't know where she got it from.

Papa was late for lunch, and I remember we ate all the bread as we waited for him and then we were worried that he'd be cross that we hadn't left any for him. He wasn't – he shook out his white napkin and tucked straight into the roast beef. He ate very fast, teasing me for being such a slowcoach. He was pleased I hadn't had gas. He wanted to know all about Wandlitz school and what we'd been learning. He polished off the beef, wiped the gravy off his plate with his potato and was just about to attack a huge slice of apple strudel when he was called to the telephone. He was gone ages and so we went ahead with our puddings, because Hubi said that otherwise we might miss our train home.

When Papa came back he was as white as a ghost. He said he had terrible news. A traitor had tried to kill the Leader. Luckily they hadn't succeeded, but the Leader had been injured and others had been killed. We were to tell no one. He had to leave immediately.

We sat in silence for a moment. Then Hubi leapt up from the table. "Come on, girls, finish up. We must go." She told us not to say a thing on the train, so we looked

161

out of the window and watched the houses and the bomb sites turn into fields. You'd think it felt nice to know something that no one else knows, but it didn't.

At one point, we stopped at some signals to wait for another train to go by. The heat was unbearable. My thighs stuck to the leather seat. Hubi had brought some water to drink, but it was as warm as bath water and completely undrinkable. At last we heard the chug of the passing train. It was going really slowly. I thought I was dreaming. It was just like how I imagine the train that Granny B. and Mummy and Grandpa Friedlander took from Brussels to Berlin. The carriages had been designed for cattle rather than people and there were air gaps above the doors but no proper windows. There were faces – mostly of women, but also of little children who they were holding up – staring out of all the gaps; and hands holding out cups and jugs as if we might be able to fill them with water as they passed. Hubi told us not to look. I pretended to look at the floor but watched out of the corner of my eye. As soon as we were in the little cart heading back to Castle Lanke, I asked her who those people were. She shook her head. "Refugees? Criminals? Jews? I really don't know."

I don't think they were criminals, because criminals are usually men.

At about this time, actually it must have been in the

autumn as the weather had turned, Papa made an appeal on the radio for everyone to donate any clothes they didn't need, so that people who had lost all their things in the bombing would have something warm to wear. The British have been bombing our cities and killing thousands of innocent people and destroying their homes. I don't know how they could do it. Papa says it's because they are cowards who are scared of our soldiers and prefer to murder defenceless women and children.

We all wanted to give something to help the poor children who had lost their clothes and we talked to Hubi about what we could give and we decided that the best things would be our spare winter coats because we really didn't need them. Mummy was rather reluctant at first because they were very expensive and had been made in Norway and were real lambskin, but in the end we persuaded her that we ought to be a good example, like Papa always says, so we made up a big parcel and Mummy sent it off.

Another part of being a good example was sticking to our rations. Mummy was the worst at it. One time she even stole Heide's butter. She said she didn't, but I know she did. It must have been the end of a week, and Mummy had finished her butter ration and only had margarine left, and unexpectedly she had a visitor. It was teatime and because, of course, we didn't have any cake or biscuits, she wanted to offer her guest a little bread and butter. She sent her maid to ask if Hubi could give her a little butter from the children's rations. Hubi couldn't believe it. She told the maid that we couldn't possibly spare any butter because we had carefully planned out what we needed for each meal until the next ration came. Which was true. So the maid went back to Mummy empty-handed. We didn't think more about it, but at suppertime, when we went to get our rations from the fridge, Heide's little portion of butter was missing. Mummy said Heide must have forgotten she'd eaten it, but I know she hadn't. We each gave Heide a scrape of ours, which really meant we had so little it was like pretend butter, though at least we had plenty of jam because Cook made loads from the blackcurrants in the garden. I don't know why Mummy didn't give that to her guest, and be done with it.

In December, Uncle Leader came to tea at Castle Lanke having driven from Berlin through heavy snow. We all had to wear these matching green dresses that Mummy had had made from the old nursery curtains. We hadn't seen Uncle Leader for almost the whole war. We sat in the big hall. Cook had made a cake for the occasion but Uncle Leader didn't touch it. He had brought his own cake and even his own flask of tea. He takes every precaution, Papa says, since those traitors tried to kill him. It seemed like the war had made him very old. It was the first time we saw how his hand trembles. I kept thinking he was going to spill his tea.

When he finished his tea and cake he wiped his mouth carefully with a napkin and patted his lap for Hedda to sit on it. I felt a mixture of relief and disappointment because before the war he always chose me to sit on his lap, and I used to hate it, but I didn't like not being chosen either.

Christmas was sad, but at least we were together. Except for Harald. By now the mystery of Harald had been solved. He had been reported missing, and that's why we didn't have any letters, and Mummy thought that he might have been killed but she had kept her fears secret so that we didn't get upset. Anyway, in the end, she heard that he'd been taken prisoner – luckily by the British. They are cruel bombers but kind to their prisoners, apparently. Strange. Anyway, Mummy was much happier once she'd had that news.

On Christmas Eve Mummy made a beautiful tree – white candles and gold and silver stars. We sat by the fire and everyone sang a song or told a story or a poem. Mummy played the piano. When Hedda recited her poem Papa started to cry. Miss Shroeter had taught it to her:

> It has to get light again
> After these dark days
> Let us not ask
> If we will see it
> New light
> Will rise again.

Then we listened to Papa's Christmas broadcast on the radio, and that was full of hope too.

Day Nine in the Bunker
Monday 30 April, 1945

I can hear singing, like the voice of a sad angel. I can't hear the words. It must be the middle of the night. No guns, no shells, no party music.

***

Porridge again for breakfast. Miss Manziarly dolloped it out silently. She's got big bags under her eyes. Heide kept singing her song about the tall telephone man under her breath: "Misch, Misch, you are a fish." She always sings it when we go past the switchboard. Luckily Mr. Misch finds it funny too. He has a wide smile. Heide says she has a sore throat but that doesn't seem to stop her singing and chatting non-stop.

Mummy came but didn't fancy porridge. She showed us a National Socialist party badge that Uncle Leader gave her last night. It's a special gold one and a great honour, she says.

There was a moment of excitement when Auntie Eva and Mummy came rushing through and dived into Mummy's bedroom. I thought Auntie Eva would come to talk to us afterwards, but she just slipped back down to the Leader Bunker without even saying hello. Mummy stayed in her room for most of the morning and then she also went down to the Leader Bunker, saying she was going to see Papa.

There was no sign of anyone in the kitchen all morning. Miss Manziarly usually gives us lunch at about 12.30, but she didn't come today. Heide and Hedda wanted to go and find Mummy and Papa, but I had a feeling that they wouldn't want to be disturbed. In the end we went as far as the stairs down to the Leader Bunker and we sat on the landing looking out for someone to come. I don't know how long we were there. Hilde brought her book, and sat reading it, sucking her cheeks. The rest of us just listened. We knew that something bad must have happened for everyone to forget about lunch. Now and then we heard footsteps, doors. Very little. Constant shelling. Then suddenly we heard the clatter of someone running in high heels, frantic knocking, and Mummy, screaming:

"Let me in! My Leader, please let me in! Please!"

"Go away!"

"Please, my Leader!"

"Go!"

We heard a door slam. Loud sobs. Mummy's footsteps retreating.

Heide started crying. I held her and shushed her. Hilde put down her book and hugged up with Holde and Hedde. We listened for more. Eventually we heard the sound of more running footsteps and Mrs. Junge came breathlessly up the stairs.

"Oh my goodness, children! What are you doing here?"

"We're waiting for lunch. Where is everyone?"

"Oh, everyone's very busy today. Come on. I'll get you some lunch. I'll go and see what I can find in the kitchen. You must be starving."

"Why is everyone so busy? What's happening? What's the matter with Mummy?"

"She's fine. I think perhaps she slept badly and she's a little tired."

"Can we go and see her?"

"Not now. Sit up nicely at the table and stay in your seats whilst I find some food in the Chancellery kitchens."

"Where's Papa?"

"He's busy, I believe. Now, there should be some bread."

"Can we see Mummy and Papa?"

"I'll go and see what's in the kitchen."

She came back from the Chancellery with some

bread and butter and a jar of preserved cherries. More like a breakfast than a lunch. I hope we're not running out of food.

Mrs. Junge didn't stop talking.

"Come on, eat up. Who needs help buttering? Holde, can you pass the butter knife to Hilde? Helmut, elbows off the table. Who wants some cherries? Heide, you must eat your crusts. Eat up, there's more if you want it. Not now, Helga. It's just a very busy day. Anyone for more bread? Water? Heide? Who needs help buttering?"

I wanted to scream.

Suddenly there was a loud bang – like a shot – much closer than anything before. For a moment I thought that the Russians must have broken into the bunker, but Helmut yelled "Bullseye!", which made us all laugh, and after that Mrs. Junge was finally quiet.

Me and Hilde helped clear up the plates, and then we went to our room for our rest. That horrid bitter marzipan smell has come back. It cuts the back of your throat and makes you feel sick right to the pit of your stomach.

There was no tea with Uncle Adi and Auntie Eva today. I wasn't looking forward to it without Blondi and the puppies, but I still felt disappointed when no one came to get us.

I really want to see Mummy now.

Miss Manziarly came back to call us for supper. She

put the food on the table without saying anything: fried eggs and mashed potato. We didn't mention lunch. Then she took a tray down for Uncle Leader. Mummy came to put us to bed. She gave Heide a red silk scarf to soothe her throat. We didn't say anything about earlier. She must have had an argument with Uncle Leader. She said she had a headache and she asked me to read the bedtime story. She kissed the tops of our heads and left me in charge. I read *The Six Who Made Their Way in the World* again and we all snuggled up together. Then we turned out our own light and tried to sleep.

It turned out to be one of the noisiest nights we've had here. There was a drunken sing-song just outside our room. It seemed to go on all night. Raucous voices completely out of tune: *Everything ends, all the pain goes away, After each December comes another May...*

Over and over. Banging and laughing. *Raise high the flags! Comrades shot dead by the red* and something. *March in spirit* – loud belching – *Blood red roses...* I tried to keep the noise out by ducking down under the covers, pulling the pillow over my ears, and going off to Swan Island with my dusty soldier boy.

1945

After Christmas it was decided that the Russian Front had got too close to Castle Lanke for safety. That's not what we were told, obviously. We were told that the house on Swan Island had been empty for too long and that it was time for us to spend some time there. I knew the real reason from listening to the servants. And from the guns. You could hear the constant rumble from the front, which the others believed was thunder.

Papa and Mummy were in Berlin. Granny B. came for lunch each day. Pickled cabbage and ham usually. Quiet meals except for Helmut's babble about Wonder Weapons and German superiority. None of the grown-ups had anything to say. Hubi gave us morning lessons – geometry and spelling and Norse myths. Miss Schroeter took the little ones. We stopped going to school because the roads were full of refugees. People fleeing from the East, escaping the Russians. Like the people on the train, they were mostly women and children. Women pushing prams piled high with blankets and pans and babies. Children in hats and overcoats dragging behind.

I couldn't get to sleep at night. I'd lie in bed for hours. I kept thinking about the refugees and the Russians, and the longer I lay there the more scared I got. I kept getting up and going to find Hubi. In the end she let me spend the evenings dozing on the sofa in the servants' sitting room. I still couldn't sleep, and I heard stories that gave me worse nightmares, but at least I didn't feel so lonely. The servants' sitting room was just off the kitchen. The cook and the maids and the governesses all sat around the kitchen table drinking beer. It was comforting to hear their chat. Until they dropped their voices, and I strained to hear the things I shouldn't know.

The servants heard their stories from the refugees, who sometimes came to the kitchen for water or food. Terrible stories. Stories of women being forced to have Russian babies. And women who were thought to be pregnant with German babies having their bellies slit open and their babies torn out. Then the Russian soldiers would smash the babies' heads against a wall or crush them under their boots. Miss Schroeter's deep voice: "They are savages. Nothing but savages."

It was during my evenings on the servants' sofa that I learnt that the Russians are likely to win the war. They have taken back all the living space that Uncle Leader had won for us in the East, but they are not stopping at the old borders. They are trying to destroy us.

I heard the servants talking about escape plans. Mr. Speer had been trying to persuade Mummy and Papa to hide us on a barge on the river. Mr. Naumann had even got a barge ready and waiting near Swan Island, stocked with food and blankets. Hubi thought we should go there, but Miss Schroeter thought it was a hopeless plan anyway. All the servants agreed that we should have been sent to Switzerland years ago. "How long will they be safe on Swan Island? A couple of months if they're lucky!" They are all making their own plans for escape. Hubi wants to stay with us, as long as she can.

In the end Head Storm Leader Schwagermann and Upper Storm Leader Rach came to fetch us. Me and Hilde helped the little ones pack. We went to say goodbye to Granny Goebbels. She was sitting quietly in her black dress. Aunt Maria sat beside her. Aunt Maria has a deep frown line just off centre between her eyes, which I've never noticed before. "What's the latest nonsense?" Granny G. asked us. We told her we were going to Swan Island. "Well, this is goodbye then." In turn we kissed her wet cheeks.

We went in two cars. Hubi came in our car. Granny B. and Miss Schroeter went with the little ones. We joined the queue of refugees, the carts and the prams. We made slow progress, waiting for people to move aside for us. A big cart got stuck in a snow drift and Head Storm Leader Schwagermann had to get out and help push. It was a relief to be moving, to be heading, at least, in the right direction, to be doing something, to be part of a big crowd. Surely the Russians could never kill this many people.

We were on Swan Island most of the time between

Christmas and Easter. There was no school because the schools there had closed. A bit like being on holiday, except Miss Schroeter and Hubi carried on teaching us in the mornings. The rest of the time we played in the garden, making snowmen and then sloshing in puddles as the snow melted. You could hear the Russian guns getting closer and closer. Granny B. kept up the pretence that it was thunder. She sighed a lot and dabbed her face with her handkerchief.

Mummy visited. She arrived with pink cheeks from the cold. Huge squeezing cuddles. There was nothing to worry about. "Uncle Leader is the best leader in the world and he will defeat his enemies. Good will prevail. It will soon be over. We will soon have peace." She put her large firm hands on my shoulders. I searched her big blue-grey eyes for evidence of whether she herself believed what she was saying. But I couldn't see through the blue.

She stayed a couple of days. It was then that Mr. Speer and his secretary visited her. Perhaps they were trying to persuade her to hide us on the barge. I don't know; what I do know is that she read to us, lined us up to sing, supervised instrument practice. I kept being hit with memories of being very young: her forcefully taking my hands to push fabric through the sewing machine, to stir heavy gingerbread dough with a wooden spoon; her being absolutely there, capable of anything and completely in charge. Somehow she'd lost this amongst the flowers of her eiderdown. We hadn't seen her strength for ages. Now it was back and for two days we had her full attention. Then she got into the black car and vanished back to Papa in Berlin. We stayed on with Hubi and Miss Schroeter and Granny B. Waiting for something. Waiting, in fact, though we didn't know it, for Mummy's telephone call summoning us to Berlin. Us being us children. Not Hubi, not Miss Schroeter, not Granny B.

She called on Hubi's day off. Miss Schroeter and Granny B. helped us pack. We were told not to bring much. We each had to choose one toy. So we knew we wouldn't be going for long. Still, I had a lump in my throat because we weren't going to be able to say good-bye to Hubi. We all chose our dolls except Helmu, who chose a toy tank. Granny B. was crying the whole time, which didn't help. "If only I could see her once more." Holde patted Granny B. on the back. "The war's nearly over, Granny B.," she said. "You can see Mummy again once the war's over."

Day Ten in the Bunker
Tuesday 1 May, 1945

A better day. The quietest morning yet. Quiet inside and hardly any shelling. Maybe this is the end, and at the eleventh hour the new troops have arrived and are pushing the Russians back.

Mummy came to get us up. She looked tired, but she had very exciting news: tomorrow we are going to Berchtesgaden! They have hired a plane with a top pilot to get us out of here. We will have an early night and go first thing tomorrow morning. I've been longing for this, but now it's come I feel sick with nerves. It will be a very dangerous journey. The little ones didn't think of that but all danced around the bedroom.

I don't know who is coming with us. Definitely Mummy and Papa and Auntie Eva and Uncle Adi, but I'm not sure what Mrs. Junge and Liesl and Miss

Manziarly are going to do. I really hope they're coming too. Especially Liesl. Surely they will because Uncle Adi and Auntie Eva will need them.

Porridge for breakfast again. Miss Manziarly was still very quiet, which made me wonder. I didn't like to ask her what her plans were. After breakfast we went to pack up all our things – we didn't need any prompting – except for our nightdresses which we'll need tonight.

We played in the corridor for a bit. There's still lots of mess from last night – champagne and schnapps and beer bottles and open cans of fruit and chocolate wrappers and ends of sausage and cigarette stubs. Charming. I don't know where the kitchen orderlies are.

We played forfeits and Mummy and Papa sat with us for a bit, but they didn't join in. I think they've got a lot on their minds with all the preparations for tomorrow. Actually, they both look quite ill. Mummy was smoking one cigarette after another, and Papa had his pulsing jaw.

It was another of those very long mornings when time seems to get stuck. We got bored of forfeits. Bored of cards. Bored of drawing. At last Miss Manziarly made us some sandwiches for lunch.

We didn't really have a rest after lunch because nobody made us. We went down to the Leader Bunker to see what was going on. There was no sign of Auntie Eva or Uncle Leader or Liesl, so no worries about getting in the way or making too much noise.

I saw the soldier boy. He came to collect a telegram from Mr. Bormann. He ran past us up the stairs, and just as he was about to go out of sight he stopped, just for a second, and looked back and smiled. He has noticed me!

We had tea with Mummy and Papa in Papa's downstairs room. Auntie Eva and Uncle Adi didn't come. There was a big chocolate cake, and only us children to eat it because Mummy and Papa weren't hungry. I think the milk must have been off again because our hot chocolate had a funny taste. None of us really wanted to drink it but Mummy said that we would need all the strength we could get for the journey tomorrow, and insisted we drink it all up.

I don't know what it was that set me off. Mummy looking so tired. Or the nasty taste of the chocolate. I got that blocked-throat feeling. I couldn't help it. I tried to hold my face, and I did, I kept it completely still, but I couldn't stop the tears. They just slipped out. I didn't wipe them away because I thought that would make everyone notice. I could taste the salt on my lips. I didn't move. Hilde was sitting beside me and was the first to notice. She actually stroked my arm and smiled.

Mummy must have seen.

"Helga," she spoke very quietly, "please."

I swallowed hard. She opened the door to take us back to our room.

"We're all going to have an early night tonight," she said. "Go to your room and get ready for bed. I'm going to fetch Dr. Kunz, so that you can have your vaccination before we go."

Heide skipped out, red scarf swinging: "Misch, Misch, you are a fish!" Big Misch gave us his usual smile, a sad smile. He opened his mouth to speak but said nothing. Everything was in slow motion. My legs felt weak. Mummy put her hand firmly on my back. "Come on, Helga, pull yourself together."

We put on our night things and were only just ready when we heard the click of Mummy's shoes in the corridor. She came in with Dr. Kunz.

Dr. Kunz is completely grey. His clothes are grey, his hair is grey, his skin is grey. He looks nervous. He is holding a black bag and his hand is shaking.

Mummy says, "Helga will go first." She comes to me and gives me a little chocolate and a kiss. She has one for each of us. In a moment she's gone.

The Goebbels family, 1942.
Top row: Josef, Hilde, Helga, Harald
Front row: Helmut, Holde, Magda, Heide, Hedda.

Postscript

On 3 May, 1945, Soviet troops entered Hitler's bunker and found the bodies of the six Goebbels children lying in their beds. They were wearing their white nightclothes and the girls had ribbons in their hair.

The story of the end of their lives has been pieced together from the testimonies of those from the Bunker who survived.

On 30 April, 1945 Hitler ate his last meal with Miss Manziarly, Mrs. Junge and his other secretaries. At the end of the meal he stood up and announced, "The time has come; it's all over." He went to talk to Goebbels who tried to persuade him to leave Berlin. Hitler insisted that his mind was made up, but encouraged Goebbels to try to escape. Goebbels said he would not abandon his Fuhrer.

The adult residents of the bunker lined up for a formal farewell. Both Hitler and Eva Braun urged everyone to try and escape. The two of them then withdrew to Hitler's sitting room. Magda Goebbels suddenly broke down in tears, and demanded to see the Fuhrer. Reluctantly he agreed. She begged him to attempt escape. He refused and she retreated, weeping.

That afternoon Adolf Hitler and his wife Eva Braun sat down on his little sofa. It is believed that she took a cyanide capsule and that he simultaneously took cyanide and shot himself in the temple. He had left instructions for their bodies to be burnt.

The following day Magda Goebbels made arrangements for her children to be killed. Helmut Kunz, a dentist, had agreed to inject the children with morphine, but he refused to help any further. According to some reports, Magda Goebbels then tried to put the cyanide capsules in the mouths of her sleeping children herself, but was unable to bring herself to do it. She sent for Dr. Stumpfegger. They went into the children's bedroom together. She may have helped him by holding each child's mouth open in turn as he crushed open a small vial of hydrogen cyanide and tipped it down their throats. This was the fatal drug that smelt of marzipan and had been tested on the dogs, and used the previous day by Eva Braun.

According to the autopsies carried out by the Soviet doctors, the children's bodies were unmarked, except for Helga's. She had suffered bruising to the face, indicating that force had been needed to get her to swallow the cyanide.

Letter from Dr. Josef Goebbels to his stepson, Harald Quandt, 28 April, 1945

Begun in the Fuhrer's bunker   28 April '45

My dear Harald,
We are now confined to the Fuhrer's bunker in the
Reich Chancellery and are fighting for our lives and
our honour. God alone knows what the outcome of
this battle will be. I know, however, that we shall
only come out of it, dead or alive, with honour and
glory. I hardly think that we shall see each other
again. Probably, therefore, these are the last lines
you will ever receive from me. I expect from you that,
should you survive this war, you will do nothing but
honour your mother and me. It is not essential that
we remain alive in order to continue to influence
our people. You may well be the only one able to
continue our family tradition. Always act in such a
way that we need not be ashamed of it. Germany
will survive this fearful war but only if examples are
set to our people enabling them to stand on their feet
again. We wish to set such an example. You may be
proud of having such a mother as yours. Yesterday
the Fuhrer gave her the Golden Party Badge which
he has worn on his tunic for years and she deserved

it. *You should have only one duty in future: to show yourself worthy of the supreme sacrifice which we are ready and determined to make. I know that you will do it. Do not let yourself be disconcerted by the worldwide clamour which will now begin. One day the lies will crumble away of themselves and the truth will triumph once more. That will be the moment when we shall tower over all, clean and spotless, as we have always striven to be and believed ourselves to be.*

Farewell, my dear Harald. Whether we shall ever see each other again is in the lap of the gods. If we do not, may you always be proud of having belonged to a family which, even in misfortune, remained loyal to the very end to the Fuhrer and his pure sacred cause.

All good things and my heartfelt greetings
Your Papa

Letter from Magda Goebbels to her son Harald Quandt, 28 April, 1945

Written in the Fuhrer's bunker   28 April '45

My beloved Son,
We have now been here, in the Fuhrer's bunker, for six days – Papa, your six little brothers and sisters and I – in order to bring our National-Socialist existence to the only possible and honourable conclusion. I do not know whether you will receive this letter. Perhaps there is still one human soul who will make it possible for me to send you my last greetings. You should know that I have remained here against Papa's will, that only last Sunday the Fuhrer wanted to help me escape from here. You know your mother – we are of the same blood, so I did not have to reflect for one moment. Our splendid concept is perishing and with it goes everything beautiful, admirable, noble and good that I have known in my life. The world which will succeed the Fuhrer and National Socialism is not worth living in and for this reason I have brought the children here too. They are too good for the life that will come after us and a gracious God will understand me if I myself give them release from it. You will go on living and

I have one single request to make of you: never forget you are a German, never do anything dishonourable and ensure that by your life our death is not in vain.

The children are wonderful. They make do in these very primitive conditions without any help. No matter whether they sleep on the floor, whether they can wash or not, whether they have anything to eat and so forth – never a word of complaint or a tear. Shell-bursts are shaking the bunker. The grown-ups protect the little ones, whose presence here is to this extent a blessing that from time to time they can get a smile from the Fuhrer.

Yesterday evening the Fuhrer took off his Golden Party Badge and pinned it on me. I am happy and proud. God grant that I retain the strength to do the last and most difficult thing. We have only one aim in life now – to remain loyal to the Fuhrer unto death; that we should be able to end our life together with him is a gift of fate for which we would never have dared hope.

Harald, my dear – I give you the best that life has taught me: be true – true to yourself, true to mankind, true to your country – in every respect whatsoever.

It is hard to start a fresh sheet. Who knows whether I shall complete it but I wanted to give you so much love, so much strength and take from you all sorrow at our loss. Be proud of us and try to remember us with pride and pleasure. Everyone must die one day and is it not better to live a fine, honourable, brave but short life than drag out a long life of humiliation?

The letter must go — Hanna Reitsch is taking it. She is flying out once more. I embrace you with my warmest, most heartfelt and most maternal love.

My beloved son
Live for Germany!
Your Mother

Who's Who

(In alphabetical order of name in text.) Any characters who do not appear on this list are fictional.

Albert Speer, 1905-1981, was Hitler's chief architect, and designer of Nazi rallies. As Armaments Minister he organised Germany's war machine using forced labour. He is famous for apologising at the Nuremberg Trials. There has been much controversy about how much he knew about the murder of Jews. He was imprisoned in Spandau until 1966, where he measured the prison's garden and walked 31,936 kilometres around it, imagining he was walking around the world, the detailed terrain in his mind's eye.

Angelica Kauffmann, 1741-1807, was a Swiss-Austrian painter and friend of Joshua Reynolds, whose work Hitler admired. Popular in her own lifetime, her reputation has declined.

Auntie Emmy, the High Lady – Emma Goering, née Sonnemann, 1893-1973, was an actress before marrying Hermann Goering. At the end of the war she spent one year in prison as a punishment for being a Nazi. She spent the rest of her life living in a small flat in Berlin.

Auntie Maria – Maria Kimmich, née Goebbels, 1910-1949, was Josef Goebbels' younger sister. She was married to the German film director Max Kimmich.

Blondi – Hitler's Alsatian, was killed in the bunker together with her puppies, to test the batch of cyanide that Eva Braun would later use to kill herself.

Dara – Gerda Christian, née Daranowski, 1913-1997, was a former model and one of Hitler's secretaries. She escaped the bunker on 1 May, 1945. She became a leading neo-Nazi and spent the rest of her life in Dusseldorf.

Dr. Kunz – Helmut Kunz was an SS dentist who is believed to have injected the children with morphine prior to their poisoning, although he is said to have refused to poison them himself. It is not known what became of him.

Dr. Stumpfegger – Ludwig Stumpfegger, 1910-1945, was an SS doctor who became Hitler's personal doctor in 1944. He helped Magda administer cyanide to the sleeping children. He died escaping from the bunker, possibly committing suicide by taking cyanide himself.

Edda Goering – b. 1938, she was the only child of Hermann and Emmy Goering and is still alive. She is said to be a lifelong Nazi supporter. Her birth was celebrated by a 500-plane flyover of Berlin. Hermann Goering allegedly boasted that he would have ordered 1000 planes if Edda had been a boy.

Empire Marshall Goering – Uncle Hermann, 1893-1946, was head of the German Air Force. He was famed for his extravagance, his drug addiction and his accumulation of wealth and body fat during the Nazi period. He was convicted of war crimes and crimes against humanity at the Nuremberg Trials and committed suicide the night before he was due to be hanged.

Ernst Speer, b. 1943, was the youngest of the Speer's six children, all of whom survived the war.

Flight Captain Reitsch – Hanna Reitsch, 1912-1979 was a record-breaking pilot said to be Hitler's favourite personal pilot. After flying out of Berlin, she was captured by the Americans with von Greim and held for eighteen months. During this time, her father killed her mother, sister and sister's children after they were expelled from their home in Poland. After her release Reitsch continued to fly. Some of her gliding records are still unbroken.

Frederick the Great – King Friedrich II of Prussia, 1712-1786.

General Field Marshall Rommel, 1891-1944, known

as the Desert Fox, for his cunning tactics in North Africa in World War II. He was famous for defying orders to kill Jewish prisoners of war. He was suspected of involvement in the plot to kill Hitler of 20 July, 1944 and was forced to commit suicide.

General Robert Ritter von Greim, 1892-1945, was a Field Marshal, pilot and the last Head of the German Air Force, when Hitler replaced Goering with him at the very end of the war. He committed suicide after being captured by the Americans in May, 1945.

Georg Schertz, b. 1935, went on to become President of the Berlin police. He has lived his whole life on Schwanenwerder (Swan Island) where he first met Helmut Goebbels.

Gerda, this is a fictional name for an unknown maid whom Magda sacked for attempting suicide.

Grandpa Friedlander, b.?-1939, was the boyfriend of Magda's mother, Auguste Behrend. They separated around the time of Magda's marriage to Gunther Quandt in 1921. He is believed to have visited Goebbels to try to get dispensation from anti-Jewish legislation, but to have been rejected. He was probably sent to Buchenwald in 1938, where he is believed to have died in 1939.

Grandpa Ritschel – Oskar Ritschel, died 1941, was Magda's father. He was probably never married to her mother and they separated when Magda was very young. He was an engineer and businessman. He is said to have introduced Magda to Buddhism.

Granny Behrend – Granny B., Auguste Behrend, 1879-?, was Magda Goebbels' mother. She survived the war. She was never able to discover what the Russians did with her grandchildren's bodies.

Granny Goebbels – Katharina Maria Goebbels, née Odenhausen, was a Dutch Roman Catholic, from a poor farming background. She survived the war.

Grete Speer – Margret Speer, b. 1938, was the second daughter of Albert and Margret.

Gretl – Gretl Fegelein, née Braun, 1915 -1987, was Eva Braun's sister. She gave birth to Fegelein's daughter on 5 May, 1945, a week after his death and a few days after Eva's. She called her daughter Eva.

Gunther Quandt, 1881-1954, was Magda Goebbels' first husband and the father of Harald. He founded an industrial empire which today includes BMW. He had two sons from his first marriage, Helmut and Herbert. Magda was rumoured to be in love with

Helmut, who was much closer to her in age than her husband. Helmut died in her arms of appendicitis when he was nineteen years old. Magda and Gunther divorced two years later.

Hans Silverstein, b.? - 1915, a Jewish soldier who was killed fighting for Germany in the First World War.

Harald Quandt, 1921-1967, was Magda Goebbels' only son from her first marriage to Gunther Quandt. He served in the German Air Force during the war and was injured and captured by the British in Italy in 1944. He was released in 1947. In 1954, he and his half-brother inherited their father's industrial empire, becoming two of the richest men in Germany. He married and had five daughters. He died in an air crash.

Head Storm Leader Schwagermann – Gunther Schwagermann, 1915- ?, was adjutant to Josef Goebbels. He left the bunker on the evening of 1 May, 1945 and escaped to West Germany, where he was held by the Americans until 1947. What happened to him after that is unknown.

Hedda – Hedwig Johanna, the second youngest of the Goebbels children, was born in 1938. She was killed in the bunker just before her seventh birthday.

Heide – Heidrun Elisabeth, the youngest of the Goebbels children, was born in 1940. She was four years old when she was killed.

Helga – Helga Suzanne, the narrator of the story, was born in 1932 and was twelve years old when she was killed.

Helmut – Helmut Christian, the only son of the Goebbels, was born in 1935. He was nine years old when he was killed.

Hilde – Hildegard Traudl, the second oldest of the Goebbels children, was born in 1934. She was just eleven when she was killed.

Holde – Holdine Kathrin, the fourth child of the Goebbels, was born in 1937. She was eight when she was killed in the bunker.

Horst Caspar, 1913-1952, was the star of the 1945 propaganda film, *Kohlberg*.

Hubi – Kathe Hubner, later Leske, was governess to the older Goebbels children between 1943 and 1945. She survived the war.

Lida – Lida Baarova, 1914-2000, was a Czech actress and star of the German film industry who had an affair with Josef Goebbels, which ended with her deportation on Hitler's orders in 1938. At the end of the war she was imprisoned for a year in Czechoslovakia for her Nazi past. After her release she continued to make occasional films. She never regretted her affair.

Liesl – Anneliese, Eva Braun's personal maid. In a letter Eva Braun wrote to her sister Gretl from the bunker on 23 April, 1945, she says "My faithful Liesl will not leave me." I am very grateful to Elizabeth Humphris for the information that her surname was Ostertag and that she survived the war.

Margret Speer – Margarete Speer, née Weber, 1905-198?, wife of Albert Speer.

Miss Braun/Auntie Eva – Eva Braun, Hitler's girlfriend and, finally, wife, 1912-1945. She committed suicide by taking a cyanide capsule on the afternoon of 30 April in Hitler's sitting room. The children would never have known this.

Miss Flegel – Erna Flegel, 1911-2006, was a Red Cross nurse. She stayed in the bunker during the Soviet capture, and went on to live a long and quiet life.

Miss Kempf – Annemarie Kempf, née Wittenberg, 1914-1991, was Albert Speer's secretary until the end of the war. When Albert Speer failed to persuade Magda

Goebbels to try to save her children and send them to the barge, he sent Annemarie Kempf to speak to her, in the hope that Magda would listen to a woman. She did not. After the war Annemarie Kempf devoted her life to looking after disabled children.

Miss Manziarly – Constanze Manziarly, Hitler's cook. She was last seen being led into a subway bunker by two German soldiers, having escaped from the bunker on the evening of the 1 May, 1945. After Hitler's suicide, she continued to cook meals for him in order to hide his death from all but his inner circle in the bunker.

Miss Schroeter – governess to the younger Goebbels children.

Mr. Bormann – Martin Bormann, 1900-1945, was Hitler's private secretary. He died escaping the bunker, probably committing suicide by taking a cyanide capsule. His wife died of cancer the following year, leaving their nine children orphaned.

Mr. Himmler – Heinrich Himmler, 1900-1945, was head of the SS, and coordinated the killing of millions of Jews. He committed suicide in 1945, after being captured by the British.

Mr. Leske – Herbert Leske was married to Kathe Hubner. Four years after the war ended she learnt that he had been killed in action.

Mrs. Junge – Traudl Junge, born Gertraud Humps, 1920-2002, was Hitler's secretary from 1943 to 1945. She escaped from the bunker on the evening of 1 May and survived the war. Her memoir, *Until the Final Hour*, has been an important source of information for this book.

Mr. Misch – Rochus Misch, b.1917, was the telephone operator in the bunker. He escaped from the bunker on 2 May, 1945 but was captured by the Russians and held prisoner in the Russian gulags until 1954. In 2005, when the Holocaust Memorial was opened in Berlin, he called for a memorial plaque for the Goebbels children at the site of the bunker and was widely criticised. He is the last survivor of the bunker.

Mr. Naumann – Werner Naumann, 1909-1982, was one of Goebbels' secretaries in the propaganda ministry. Magda Goebbels is believed to have been in love with him in 1944, but after a warning from Goebbels, he distanced himself from her. He escaped from the bunker on 1 May, 1945, and went on to become director of a metal factory owned by Magda's son Harald.

Mummy – Magda Goebbels, 1901–1945. After killing her children, she went down to the lower bunker in tears, and played patience. She then went with Josef Goebbels to the garden of the Reich Chancellery, where they both committed suicide. She took cyanide.

Papa – Josef Goebbels, 1897-1945, was Hitler's propaganda chief. He shot himself in the garden of the Reich Chancellery on 1 May, 1945. When the Russians entered the bunker compound on 3 May, his charred corpse was found beside his wife's body. There had not been enough petrol to burn the bodies totally.

Reggie – Regine Goldschmidt, 1924-1944, was the daughter of Samuel Goldschmidt, the Jewish banker and neighbour of the Goebbels family on Schwanenwerder (Swan Island) whose property Josef Goebbels appropriated. The Goldschmidt family fled to France, where Samuel Goldschmidt died in 1940. Regine was presumably deported, for she died in Auschwitz. All details about her have been imagined.

State Secretary Hanke – Karl Hanke, 1903-1945, worked in Goebbels' propaganda ministry. He is believed to have had an affair with Magda Goebbels in 1938. He is thought to have been executed by Czechs or Poles in 1945.

The dusty soldier boy – the young soldier boy who dropped the glass was Armin D. Lehmann, b. 1928-2008, and was the author of *In Hitler's Bunker,* in which he recalls the incident with the glass. He was a boy soldier in the bunker working as a courier. He escaped on 1 May, 1945. He was a lifelong peace campaigner. He emigrated to the US in 1953 and worked in California as a professor of tourism. His significance to Helga is imagined.

The Leader – Uncle Leader, Uncle Adi – Adolf Hitler, 1889-1945, was Chancellor of Germany from 1933 to 1945. On the afternoon of 30 April, 1945 he and Eva Braun withdrew to his sitting room in the lower bunker. Sitting next to each other on the sofa, he shot himself in the head; she took a cyanide capsule. The children never learnt of their deaths.

Upper Group Leader Fegelein – Hermann Otto Fegelein, 1906-1945. He was a General of the Waffen SS. He married Eva Braun's sister Gretl in 1944. He left the bunker and was caught drunk in his Berlin flat and accused of trying to flee. He is believed to have been executed on 29 April, 1945 on Hitler's orders.

Upper Storm Leader Rach – Gunther Rach – a Nazi driver (dates unknown). It is not known what became of him.

Victor (Chaim) Arlosoroff, 1899-1933, was a Russian-born Zionist with whom Magda had an affair before, and probably during, her first marriage. His sisters, Lisa Arlosoroff-Steinberg and Dora Arlosoroff, were Magda's close teenage friends. Victor was murdered in Palestine in 1933. Memorial services were held for him in cities throughout the world, including Berlin.

Wilfried von Oven, 1912-2008, was press officer for Josef Goebbels. He was born and died in South America.

A note on names

All personal titles and those place names which lend themselves to interpretation have been translated into English to give a sense of their meaning to Helga.

Acknowledgements

My first acknowledgement is to the film *Downfall*, which inspired this book. I have also drawn on lots of books, principally:

Angela Lambert, *The Lost Life of Eva Braun* (2006).
Anja Klabunde, *Magda Goebbels* (2001).

Anonymous, *A Woman in Berlin* (2000).

Armin D. Lehmann with Tim Carroll, *In Hitler's Bunker* (2004).

Bernd Freytag von Loringhoven, *In the Bunker with Hitler* (2005).

David Irving, *Goebbels. Mastermind of the Third Reich* (1996).

Gitta Sereny, *Albert Speer: His Battle with Truth* (1995).

H.R. Trevor-Roper, *Hitler's Table Talk* (1953).

Hans-Otto Miessner, *Magda Goebbels* (1980).

Ian Kershaw, *Hitler*, 2 vols (1998, 2000).

Joachim Fest, *Inside Hitler's Bunker* (2004).

Marie Vassiltchikov, *The Berlin Diaries 1940-1945* (1999).

Martin Gilbert, *The Holocaust* (1986).

Nicholas Stargardt, *Witnesses of War* (2006).

Petra Fohrmann, *Die Kinder des Reichsministers* (2005) translated for me by Sonja Laue.

Ralf Georg Reuth, *Goebbels* (1993).

Traudl Junge with Melissa Muller, *Until the Final Hour* (2003).

Various editions of Josef Goebbels' diaries.

I also made use of Google and Wikipedia for links to the Goebbels' home movies.

I'd like to thank everyone who gave me and lent me books and films or pointed me in the right direction –

Sasha and Anna Gunin, William Rees-Mogg, Charlotte Rees-Mogg, Jo Glanville, Miranda Cresswell, Tom Weldon, Rebecca Nicolson. Thanks also to Alan Judd for his advice and to Tom Flatt for his thoughts about wolves. I also want to thank Anja Toddington and Sonja Laue for their help with translation. I have hugely benefited from Sonja's imaginative involvement with this project. A big thank you to my aunt Elizabeth Bruegger for sharing her memories of life in a Nazi family in 1938 and for requesting and translating the personal memories of Hildegard Forstermann, to whom I am also very grateful. Thanks also to Rudolf Kortokraks for sharing his memories of his German childhood. Thank you to Jonny White, Charlotte Rees-Mogg, Kate Hubbard and David Craigie for reading drafts. Thank you to Rebecca Nicolson and Emily Fox for their enthusiasm and to Aurea Carpenter and Vanessa Webb for their constructive and detailed engagement with the text. Thank you to Tom Baldwin for the great title. Thanks to Jess Bell for all her neighbourly support. Love and thanks to my parents for all their support. Big love and thanks to David for his encouragement and to Maud, Wilf, Myfanwy and Samuel for bearing so much talk of the Nazis.